RISE OF THE PAGANS

Jesse S. Smith

Basementia Publications
Silverton, Oregon

Rise of the Pagans
Jesse S. Smith

Published by Basementia Publications
Silverton, Oregon

Cover design by Jesse S. Smith

ISBN 978-0-9766423-8-1

First edition August 4, 2014
Second edition June 10, 2016
Third edition November 15, 2020

Visit **www.riseofthepagans.com**

Fiction

Introduction

Before casting the spell, I must make a note about spelling.

For the convenience of the reader, and with apologies to purists, I have substituted simplified phonetic spellings in place of the sometimes convoluted Gaelic names for the Pagan holidays.

I used Sowan instead of Samhain; Immolc rather than Imbolc, Imbolg, or Oimell; and Brigid in place of Brighid. I generally stuck with Ostara for the holiday and Eostar for the goddess. I used Lunasa instead of Lughnasadh (but more often, Lammas).

I hope this convention will make the story more accessible without detracting from its meaning.

The incident described in this book as the "Lammas Attack" was inspired by actual real-life events that occurred at the Anarchists' Beltane at Stinson Flats in Cougar National Forest, Washington, in May of 2005 (and again in 2006).

All other events are products of the author's imagination; and none of the characters in this story are intended to represent actual persons, living or passed.

Chapter I: A New Perspective

"I hate Mondays," sighs Hayden to no one in particular, as he gazes out the window at the rain pounding down on the gray world outside.

"The day of the Moon," comments his co-worker Nicholas, who is more optimistic.

A flock of birds breaks screaming overhead. Nobody notices.

"What?" asks Hayden distractedly. His large, worried eyes peer at Nicholas tiredly from below his unkempt hair.

"The Moon," Nicholas repeats. "Moon Day. Monday. It's where the word comes from."

"Really?" says Hayden, who does not care. "I never thought about it."

"Sure," explains birdlike Nicholas, flapping his arms as he speaks. "The days of the week are all named in the old Pagan tradition." His beak of a nose dips back into his coffee cup.

"They are?" Hayden has been trying to read the news on his smartphone, but the news is so bad, he can barely get past the headlines. Now he looks up at Nicholas, and decides that he is grateful for any diversion.

"Well, yeah," Nicholas explains. "Western culture is largely based on Pagan tradition. That's why the week begins with Sun Day, the day of the Sun. Followed by Moon Day, the day of the Moon. Tuesday is Tyr's Day, named for a Viking battle god. Wednesday is Wodin's Day. Odin, as you know, was the king of all the Norse gods. We get Thursday from Thor's Day, named for the famous god of thunder. And Friday is Freya's Day,[1] named after a beautiful goddess."

"But Saturday is just Saturn Day, like the planet," observes Hayden.

"It's Saturn Day," agrees Nicholas. "But the planet Saturn was named for the Roman god of agriculture and prosperity."

Hayden is thinking of the ancient empire, its aristocratic traditions, its culture of unabashed militaristic expansionism. "The Roman gods," he says. "Of course. They live on in the cultures of the conquered."

"Well, if you prefer, you could think of our days of the week as sharing the names of the planets of the Solar System. It could help you get through the week, if you go in for that sciencey sort of thing."

"Sure," says Hayden. "Sunday, Monday... wait, what planet is Tuesday?"

"Well, it works better in a true Romance language, like Spanish, or French," explains Nicholas. "Those languages still use their variants on the old Roman names for the days of the week."

"French?"

"Right. *Oui.* So, the French weekdays are *lundi, mardi, mercredi, jeudi, vendredi, samedi,* and *dimanche.*"

Hayden is listening, so Nicholas explains:

"*Lundi,* from the Latin *luna,* the Moon, Moon Day, Monday. *Mardi* is Mars Day..."

"Wait," interrupts Hayden. "You memorized all this?"

"Sure," replies Nicholas. "In high school. Next is

---

[1] Or "Frigg's Day"

Tuesday. In French the word is *mardi*, or Mars Day; named for the Roman god of War, or the Red Planet, if you prefer. After that comes *mercredi*, or Mercury Day. Thursday is *jeudi*, for Jove's Day, Jupiter's Day, the gas giant of our solar system, named after the king of the Gods, the Roman equivalent of Zeus.

"Then comes v*endredi*, Venus Day, our Friday. After that is *samedi*, for Saturn Day, our Saturday."

"Yeah?" prods Hayden. "What about Sunday?"

"Well for us it's Sun Day, the day of the Sun. In French they call it *dimanche*, which is just some Abramist imposition of cultural imperialism."

"What was that?" asks Hayden, who thinks he has heard wrong.

"I'm talking quietly," explains Nicholas, "because, well, I don't like to offend people, and most of the folks around here are Abramists."

"Abramists?"

"Yeah. You know. Followers of the religion of Abraham, or its offshoots: Judaism, Christianity, Islam, Baha'i, and so on."

Hayden feels a wave of understanding and recognition wash over him.

"It's funny, isn't it," continues Nicholas, "that the world's dominant religions – the Christians, the Muslims, and the Jews – are all based on the beliefs of a guy who worshiped a spirit embodied in a pile of rocks and a creosote bush. It all sounds sort of Pagan, when you think about it."

"Huh. Yeah, I hear that Paganism is sort of a thing again."

"Yeah. You know, there's an active Pagan community, right here in this town."

"No shit," says Hayden. "Really?" He is thinking to

himself that the only Pagans he has seen are the dirty savages from Hollywood movies. They always attack in hordes, to viciously overwhelm the righteous Christians or the loyal Roman legionnaires. It is difficult to shake the image.

"You a religious man, Hayden?" Nicholas asks, with a look that anticipates the answer.

"Not particularly," our hero answers confidentially. "I've been to church lots when I was a kid, but these days I prefer science. Scientific facts. You know, physics, astronomy, chemistry, biology, and evolution."

"Ah, well then," says Nicholas proudly. "Paganism is the perfect philosophy for a man of science. It's the only religion that overtly celebrates the Solstices and Equinoxes."

"That's cool."

"The Summer Solstice, as you know, is the longest day of the year. For us here, it is the point in the Earth's orbit where the Northern Hemisphere is closest to the Sun."

"Right."

"And the Winter Solstice, of course, is the opposite point in the Earth's orbit: the longest night of the year. After the Winter Solstice, the nights get shorter. No matter how bad the winter gets, after the Winter Solstice you know that at least the days are getting longer, the winter is not eternal, things will get better. It's a form of renewal, a time of new beginnings, a source of hope in the long dark night. That's why the Winter Solstice has always been so important to people. The event of the Winter Solstice and its cultural significance were so important that the Abramists could not ban its observance. Instead they had to co-opt the holiday, if they were to have any hope of gaining acceptance in continental Europe."

"—And the Equinoxes are the midway points between the Solstices," interjects Hayden, who already knows all this, being a man of science and all.

"Exactly! The Equinoxes are when the day and the night are of equal lengths, hence equinox, meaning equal night, right? You got it!" Nicholas says encouragingly, if perhaps a tad patronizingly. He continues:

"So the primary Pagan holidays are the Solstices, the Equinoxes, and the days midway between the Solstices and Equinoxes. Some sects also have ceremonies based on the phases of the moon," Nicholas continues. "Pagans pay their respects to the forces of Nature; the Earth itself. She is Mother Earth, the Earth Mother, the Goddess, the bringer of life. She is often paired with her consort, the Horned God, Pan, bringer of pandemonium, because life is sustained by chaos and death. Or you could pair her with the Sun god if you prefer. The ancients didn't limit the Goddess to a single mate."

"But that's just it," Hayden objects. "Doesn't Paganism involve lots of gods and goddesses? How is that scientific?"

"Oh, well, that's easy! If you're of a more sort of analytical mindset then you just explain the gods and goddesses as archetypes and metaphors: symbols for forces of nature and human concerns."

"But surely, not everyone thinks of all the gods and goddesses as a metaphor."

"Oh, not at all! But we don't have big gatherings just to talk about dogma. Whether they think of the Goddess and Magic and all the various gods and myths as allegorical metaphor or literal Truth, the one great thing that draws everyone together is the rituals, the festivals, the celebrations of the sacred rites. Our common denominator is that we celebrate the movement of the sun and the moon: the seasons, the Sabbats, the Solstices and Equinoxes and all the myriad historical connotations imparted unto them.

"There are certainly Pagans," he goes on, "who think of the multitude of divinities in literal terms, as spirits who inhabit the earth and the trees and the clouds and the oceans and the sun. And some are so devoted to the cult of The Goddess that they're practically monotheistic. But I think many Pagans consider the gods to be like Jungian archetypes. Gods are metaphysical representations of the physical manifestations of the forces of nature. The myths surrounding them are manifestations of the human consciousness and the individual's state of being within a complex human society."

"Really?"

"Why not? It works perfectly. There's a deity for every state of mind and a hundred myths for every strong emotion. There's even a spirit for every grotto and knoll, a nymph for every tree, a dryad for every creek and spring. Many local deities are a sort of abstraction of the power of a place. Which ancient tradition do you want to draw from? Take your pick. The Norse, the Celts, the African tribes, the Babylonians, the Greeks, they were all Pagans of one kind or another, even if they didn't use the word 'Pagan' to describe themselves."

"Pagan just means not Christian, doesn't it?"

"Well to some, maybe. In the modern era the word Paganism has come to denote a polytheistic philosophy, involving worship of the natural elements. To many people, it's effectively the same as Wicca."

"Yeah, I've heard of the Wikkans," says Hayden.

"The Wiccans are by far the largest subset of modern Paganism," Nicholas explains. "But I would argue that Wicca is just one way of practicing Paganism. There are many other possibilities. Wicca is one expression of Paganism, with its own dogmas and traditions, in the same way that Greek

Orthodoxy, Bible Belt Baptist, Hasidic Judaism and Sunni Islam are all expressions of Abramism."

"You don't approve of Wiccans?"

"I love Wiccans. Many of my friends are Wiccans. I just don't happen to be a Wiccan myself. I'm more of a Hermeticist, personally."

At this point, they have to go back to work. They continue the conversation that evening, over beers at a local hangout.

"The best part about Paganism is the Pagan holidays," says Nicholas. "We call them Sabbats."

"The Sabbats... like, the Sabbath?"

"Yes, like the witches' Sabbats; courtesy of the Middle Ages. The word derives from the same root as the word the Abramists use: a word that means 'seven' in the old Semitic dialects."

"Right, like the Sabbath, the seventh day of the week," says Hayden, who did go to church with his parents while he was growing up.

"Yeah! But it's sort of a misnomer, because there are actually eight Pagan Sabbats. These holy days divide the year into perfect segments, like the way you'd cut a pizza: half, quarters, eighths. We call them the quarters and the cross-quarters.

"The quarters are the solar holidays: the Solstices and Equinoxes. The cross-quarter days are midway between the quarters; so they are the earth holidays: the changing of the seasons, the harvest, lambing, planting, and so on. Well, theoretically they're midway. In practice, we've allowed tradition to fix the dates of the cross-quarters, so they are sometimes several days off of where they should be, according to a proper solar calculation."

"So, I know," interjects Hayden, "that the Winter Solstice

is the same holiday as Christmas, and that it's based on an ancient Pagan holiday. But I don't know about the other pagan holidays."

"Oh, but you do," replies Nicholas. "You just didn't know they were Pagan. Take Valentine's Day, for example. That's based on the old Roman festival of Lupercalia, which was an important fertility rite."

"So is Valentine's Day one of the Sabbats?"

"No, it's just an extra holiday. You can have all the holidays you want in a year; but there are only the eight Sabbats."

"OK, so what are they, then?"

"First, well, as you were saying, you've got Yule, the Winter Solstice, which the Abramists call Christmas. It's the rebirth of the year, the longest night of the year, as dark as the winter will get, and after that things can only get better."

"Sure."

"Next there's Immolc, the cross-quarter day on February 2. It's a celebration of the coming of Spring, a feast day dedicated to the goddess Brigid. The name Immolc is from 'ewe's milk' because it's the feast of the first lambing. In the Arthurian legends, the Abramists called it Candlemas; but our modern culture has trivialized it to lousy Groundhog's Day. Don't be fooled. As a day of holy observance, Immolc has ancient roots.

"This is followed by the Vernal Equinox, the springtime equilibrium between night and day. We call it Ostara, the Pagan rite of Spring. The holiday is named after a popular fertility goddess, Eostar. She is the true origin of the holiday that the Abramists call Easter. The bunnies and the eggs are obvious fertility symbols from the Pagan tradition.

"The fourth Sabbat is Beltane, the 'favoring fire' of Druid

magic, the fertility ritual with the well-known ancient Pagan tradition of dancing 'round the Maypole."

"And the May Queen?"

"All that drama. Yes. These days, the holiday is commonly known as May Day. The Eastern Europeans call it Walpurgisnacht."

"Oh, is that what that is." He thinks for a moment, then asks, "So tell me, why are Pagans so obsessed with fertility?"

"Well you've got to remember, fertility is the oldest form of wealth. In the olden days, if you had more children, then you had more workers, and your farm could produce more. If your livestock were fertile, then you had more livestock to eat or milk or sell or plow your fields. If your fields were fertile, you had more food. Abundance could get you through the winter. So praying for fertility is in many ways a wish for prosperity."

"Prosperity. Very modern."

"Yes, we could all do with some prosperity."

"All right, so go on."

Nicholas continues: "My own personal favorite holiday is Litha, the Summer Solstice: the longest day of the year, and the shortest night. Always a wild party. They say if you jump over the Litha bonfire, your wish will come true... but mine didn't.

"Anyway, next is Lunasa, the feast of the god Lugh. The Abramists call it Lammas; and really, most of us do, too. It's observed on August 1, at the height of the summer season, to celebrate the beginning of the early harvest. Lammas Day was an important harvest feast, often associated with the blessing or sacrifice of a loaf of bread. For the ancient Celts, Lughnasadh was an entire month-long summer festival. The Irish Gaels called it Bron Trogain, meaning the time when the Earth goes into labor and begins to bear the harvest fruit.

"The Fall Equinox celebrates another perfect balance between night and day, as the Earth swings around to winter time again. We often call the Fall Equinox by its neo-Pagan name, Mabon.

"Finally, to celebrate the darkening of the year, is an ending ritual, Sowan, the ritual of death, the recognition of the Dark Side as a necessary counterpart to life; the completion of the cycle, the fulfillment of the circle, the celebration of fear and darkness and the spirits of our ancestors. It is a time for memory, and a time for costumes, and for feasting on the autumn harvest. It is the time of year when days grow short and the sun seems to be dying. The wind howls and evokes the sound of ghastly spirits, causing creaks in the home. The rain and cold weather drive spiders and bats and rodents into people's houses. In short, it is a time of fear; and in their wisdom, our forebears decided to celebrate their fear of death, rather than deny it.

"So that's the origin of Sowan. These days, it is more commonly known by its Abramist name: Halloween."

"I see," says Hayden. "It makes sense that Halloween was originally a Pagan holiday."

"Sure. They all were. Almost all of our holidays are Pagan in origin." He goes on in a somewhat pedantic tone, "The Gaelic spelling for Sowan is Samhain, so you see it written like that a lot, if you read Pagan texts or old books. The name Sowan derives from the Old Gaelic for 'gentle sound', the sound of gentle voices which marked the Summer's End. In the elder calendar, Sowan was actually the end of the year, their version of New Year's Eve: the death of the year itself, when the borders of the spirit world were in flux."

"And that's it? Those are all the Pagan holidays?"

"Well, those are all the Sabbats. There are some folks who

get together for ritual every full moon. And sometimes people who are pursuing some specific sort of goal of spiritual fulfillment will even form a coven and get together every week."

"A coven, like, a witches' coven?"

"Sure. A witch is just a practitioner of magic. I'm a witch."

"You're a witch? But you're a guy!"

"A warlock then. Whatever. Modern witchcraft," explains Nicholas, "is the pursuit of a state of mind in which the practitioner is highly attuned to the universal constant in the surrounding environment. It's a transcendent state of focus akin to meditation, some forms of yoga, or deeply felt prayer. The modern practice of witchcraft may involve some herb lore, but primarily emphasizes guided imagery meditation and a focus of energetic flow."

"Not a lot of eye of newt," observes Hayden.

"No," says Nicholas. "Or toe of frog, either. Sometimes we even bust out a cauldron for ritual but, it's really just symbolic. The only potions we ever brew are tea, cider, and mulled wine; and we brew those over the stove. Well, and we make mead, of course."

"Mead... that's with honey, right?"

"Nothing but honey and water in the very best meads, a little bit of brewer's yeast to top it off. Some people like to flavor theirs with a bit of pomegranate juice. Occasionally, you'll run into somebody who likes to mix theirs with a bit of damiana tincture; that's the good stuff."

"It what?"

"It's just an herb. But the mead, depending on who makes it, it's as strong as wine, most of the time, and sometimes even stronger. There's nothing like a good dry mead. And we pass it around and do toasts. Everyone makes a toast to whatever they want to toast. Sometimes the toasts are wishes, or prayers, or praise and acknowledgement for a member of the community who has done something spectacular, performed a deed of altruism or some other kind of heroism. Sometimes the toasts get quite involved, and take the form of a dissertation, or a poetry reading. And the more mead everyone has had to drink, the lengthier the toasts get."

Suggestion is a powerful force, so the young men order another round.

"You'd love going to the festivals though," Nicholas says later. "There really are all kinds of people within the community."

"All kinds? Really? I thought it was all mostly just a bunch of hippies."

"Hippies? Do I look like a hippie to you?"

It is true. While Nicholas may look a little strange, he is not exactly what you would call a "hippie."

"I mean, yeah," Nicholas explains, "there are a lot of sort of quasi-hippies in the Pagan community. It's a cross-section of society. There's all sorts of people. There are goths, hipsters, yuppies, and punks; and plenty of just regular people. There are business owners and highly paid professionals, hanging out with manual laborers, and farmers, minimum wage workers, even people on welfare. All kinds. It is above all else egalitarian. It's not just people of one socioeconomic status, orientation, or lifestyle choice who attend. There are gays, lesbians, the polyamorous crowd, plenty of young singles on the pull, nobody cares, whatever, we're just there to celebrate together.

"And it's a family show. There are grandparents. There are lots of plain vanilla, regular families, people with children.

There are always a pack of children running around together at all the festivals. You'll see several generations, from the grandparents to the babies, all there together, dancing around the bonfire. There are nature-lovers and granola types; but we've got your typical urban youth, and some total rednecks, too."

"Really, rednecks hang out with hippies?"

"Yeah, I'm telling you, nobody cares. One of the core members of our community is Dennis. He wears a cowboy hat and shit kickers, all the time. Drives a big ol' pickup truck, the whole bit. Fantastic guy. Real salt of the earth."

"So I take it there's no particular political philosophy, either."

"Naw, man, Paganism is a religious philosophy, it's not political. We definitely don't all agree about politics. I know some real Ayn Rand-quoting libertarian anarchist nuts; we've got our socialists too.

"The Pagan community looks like American society," he continues. "Of course, there's plenty of SCA folks as well."

"SCA?" Hayden has heard the name, and almost thinks he knows what it means, but his mind is a bit slow in retrieving the words that are represented by the initials.

"You know, the Society for Creative Anachronism. The Renaissance Faire folks. The people who like to dress in medieval garb and practice swordplay. It's all about the fancy costumes, and when you see the busty maidens in their corsets and low-cut, cleavage-baring gowns... well, it's hard to complain."

"Sounds fun."

"It is. You should come sometime."

They leave the discussion there, for the time being.

A few days later, Nicholas casually mentions that he will be participating in an upcoming ritual over the weekend.

When Hayden expresses interest, Nicholas invites him to join him in attending the ritual for Beltane.

Chapter II: Beltane

Hayden carpools to Beltane with Nicholas. They pass the long drive to the festival site in idle speculation on their co-workers' sex lives, a conversation which descends into hilarity as the speculations grow increasingly creative and unlikely.

This particular Beltane festival is held in a remote location, in a secluded campground in a national forest. The scenery is spectacular, as the sun shines between the gigantic trees along a broad vista of rugged hillsides, here and there dotted with mossy boulders and giant ferns.

Once they arrive at the festival site, Nicholas introduces Hayden to a lot of people in a short time. It is a bit overwhelming. Hayden knows he will not be able to remember any of their names.

The first person to approach them is a friendly young man in his mid- to late- twenties, with deep brown skin, kinky black hair, and chiseled facial features befitting a marble statue of a Greek god. Nicholas introduces him as Phoenix.

"Good to see you," Phoenix tells Nicholas with a broad smile. "Welcome to Beltane," he says to Hayden, and Hayden feels truly welcomed.

After he moves on, Hayden asks, "Is his name really Phoenix?"

"Well," Nicholas replies, "I think his parents named him

Thomas or something, but everyone calls him Phoenix now. As I understand it, he underwent a spiritual transformation, several years ago; so the name indicates that he has been reborn from the ashes of his old self, into a new life within the Pagan community, or something like that.

"And this is Sage," Nicholas says, introducing an older woman with long grey hair, who is wearing a long flowing and very colorful print dress. Sage is adorned with a long flowing scarf, dangly earrings, several long dangly necklaces, and a number of ornate rings. Hayden notices that at least one of the rings is made from antler, and has a pentagram carved in it.

Sage greets him warmly, and says, "You know, the name 'Hayden' means 'Heathen' in Old German. You have a perfect name for a member of the Pagan community."

"My parents would be appalled," he replies with a smile.

At this point in the conversation, a couple approaches the group. Nicholas introduces them as Dennis and Diana. They are a few years older than Hayden; Diana is perhaps in her late thirties and Dennis looks to be in his early- or mid-forties. Hayden has already heard about Dennis: he's the one who wears a cowboy hat and boots, and drives a pickup truck. "Howdy," Dennis says, offering a leathery calloused hand with a firm grip.

"Dennis is the guy who gets things done around here," Nicholas explains. "Sometimes we try to help, and sometimes we just try to stay out of his way."

"Mostly they stay out of the way when I need some help," Dennis comments wryly.

"And this is Diana," says Nicholas.

"Don't worry, we don't put you to work right away," says Diana with a friendly wink. Hayden is too surprised to say anything in response; it's been quite a while since anyone winked at him. He smiles and shakes her hand.

There are many more introductions. As Nicholas had predicted, there are a number of hippies, a few goths, and a whole lot of more or less fairly normal-looking people. The group trends young. One of the hippies is Dylan, a cheerful young man with youthful features. One of the goths is Marc, who seems very serious and not particularly outgoing.

But Hayden quickly forgets about everyone else when Nicholas introduces him to a really cute, elfin-faced young woman.

"This is Melissa," says Nicholas.

"Hi," says Melissa, and flashes him a mischievous pixie grin.

Hayden smiles back and says, "Nice to meet you." He genuinely means that. He thinks that he'd like to spend some time getting to know her better.

That night, Hayden sits around a bonfire in a giant open field, and shares some red wine. He plays a borrowed hand drum for a while, then passes it on and listens to others drumming. A few of the women dance to the drums.

Melissa is one of the dancers, and after circling the fire several times, she stops and dances in place, right in front of Hayden. He knows it is rude to stare, but he cannot seem to stop watching her. She catches his eye and smiles.

She continues dancing for a while, then goes off and talks to her friend for a minute, glancing back in his direction occasionally. Finally she returns and takes a seat next to him. His heart is pounding uncontrollably, but he manages to make small talk. Her manner is entirely casual as she sits very close to him, and gradually moves in closer until they are touching. Eventually he puts his arm around her, and she leans her head on his chest, and he buries his face in her hair, and they sit there like that quietly, basking in the glow of each other's' company.

As the evening wears on, there comes a spontaneous lull in the drumming, followed by a lull in the chatter.

And as they all sit there, quietly staring into the fire, Phoenix steps up to the center of the circle, his back to the fire, and intones the following dissertation.

"In the beginning," Phoenix says, "there was nothing. Or more properly there was a big swirling eddy of the basic building blocks of the universe, the stuff that would become everything; but it was undifferentiated, amorphous, chaotic, lacking in uniqueness and originality.

"Everything was there, but it didn't really look like anything. Yet.

"Then after time the swirling spirals and eddies collapsed in on themselves, and these irregularities grew and built up so much energy that they became suns and clusters of suns and galaxies of star clusters and a whole universe filled with galaxies. Physics tells us this, astrophysics, the great temporal expostulation of mankind as we discern what exists around us and describe it to each other the way we have always done, throughout the eons, around the fire, back to the time when our ancestors were not yet creatures that we now would consider to be 'human;' nor would they be likely to accept us, had they survived to meet us, their fat, ugly, lethargic descendants. They would weep in shame to see how far we have strayed from whatever it is that they would have considered the Right Way of Being. Perhaps.

"Yet it's just as likely that the Australopithecines were in the habit of intentionally starting forest fires: to flush game; or to clear underbrush near their encampments, to maintain a perimeter that could be more easily defended against predatory animals. When it's just you and a small group, in the deep middle of a dense forest of very tall trees, you feel very small, and you notice that it's really dark, because the trees block out the moon and stars. Try it sometime. You may sympathize with our forest-burning ancestors, even if their repeated blazes in North Africa contributed to the process that transformed a swamp-filled Rain Forest wetlands into today's Sahara Desert."

At this point in Phoenix's speech, Sage steps up beside him, and interjects her own commentary.

"In this regard," she says, "mythology agrees with physics. The creation myths of many cultures speak of an undifferentiated field of some kind: to the Greeks, it was Chaos; to the Norse, it was Niflheim and Muspelheim, the twin forces of fire and ice. The Crow tribes of North America spoke of a boundless flood, from which the lands of the world emerged.

"Yet in all these myths, as in physics, some force acts on the chaos which causes order to arise out of chaos; or if not order, exactly, at least *form*, for to many of these cultures, the lands that emerged were still chaotic, a riot of life, filled with strange creatures, horrible monsters, and bizarre, inexplicable shapes and situations."

She nods at Phoenix, who goes on with his previous line of thought as best he can.

"It's interesting you mentioned the flood," he says, "because it's a common theme in cultures around the world. In this respect, the Native American peoples' creation story is not unlike the flood myth of the ancient Sumerians, which is told as part of the Epic of Gilgamesh. And if you read Gilgamesh, you notice that the flood myth reads like the retelling of a story which had already been around for a long time. The Sumerian flood myth was eventually adopted into the Abramist canon, and most of us are familiar with it as the story of Noah's Ark. A different version of the flood story found its way into Greek mythology as well, with Deucalion and Pyrrha. The theme has resonance because floods have power; and the story has lasted for so long because stories have power of their own.

"Over time, all the people of the earth told their own stories about their own gods. Gods were local, specific to a place or a tribe of people. Mythology was a way of explaining the world, and it helped to consolidate a tribal identity.

"In Africa, in Babylon, in China, in India, in ancient Egypt and South America, and even in the caves of Paleolithic Europe, the people manifested their hopes and fears, gave them names, personified them, endowed the personifications with supernatural powers and deeply human failings. The gods wielded and represented the capricious forces of nature, but stories about the gods were a mirror to the tribe, held up so they could see themselves, and perhaps analyze their own circumstances, their hopes, fears, dreams, and wild imaginings, in a more abstract perspective. Certainly the gods of most cultures are driven by rage, jealousy, lust and warmongering; so these characteristics are emblematic, or perhaps disparagingly derisive, of the societies who invented these myths.

"As time went by," he says, "and migrating cultures interacted, awkward social situations arose with disagreement about the name of the king of all the gods. Sometimes, to resolve these differences, it might be agreed that a certain god had many names, or a son. Sometimes, after the passage of much time and the evolution of society, or perhaps as the consequence of some invasion (whether an influx of migrants; an invasion of ideas brought in by merchants or mariners; or most often, a military invasion of conquest) the victor would explain that a new generation of gods had triumphed over the previous generation. In India, a mind-bogglingly complex pantheon arose, with thousands of gods and goddesses, each with many aspects and incarnations, parents and children, gods who had been sacrificed to make the world, and gods whose ultimate kingship of reality was subjected to some very creative abstraction of the definition of reality, perhaps a creative line of thought attributable to the popularity of the hallucinogenic Soma, which was reputed to endow the imbiber with mystical powers.

"In Egypt, Horace was the son of Osiris. It was the mythological murder of Osiris that cleared the way and allowed Horace to assume the kingship of heaven from his father.

"In ancient Greece, Zeus castrated his father Kronos, and the Olympians threw down the Titans.

"In Scandinavia, Odin and the Aesir supplanted the Vanir, and threw down the ugly old Jotun giants who originally ruled over Midgard.

"In Ireland, when the new Gaelic gods were ascendant, the old Pictish gods of the Tuatha De Danann were turned into the diminutive inhabitants of the Faery Realm."

Hayden glances at the dark-haired, pixie-faced girl by his side. She looks back at him with an impish grin.

"The fairies are a perfect example of gods coming full circle within a tradition; for many gods begin as a spirit that was said to inhabit a particular place or natural feature. Ancient Greece was alive with sprites, fauns, nymphs, and dryads. Pagan tradition was so deeply in touch with natural features that the Abramists actually outlawed the act of holding ceremonies at waterfalls, springs, streams, and large majestic trees. Because those waterfalls, springs, streams, and large majestic trees are the places where Pagans draw their power.

Even today, if one wanders in the Himalayas, one may encounter unique shrines tucked into many corners, groves, rocky outcroppings, sometimes even an auspicious paving stone that's been awarded a special reverence for some reason.

"Why, even the God of the Abramists began as the spirit of one particular pile of altar stones.

"Abram, who grew rich from whoring his own wife out to Pharaoh. Abram, who nearly murdered his own son because the voice in his head told him to do it. Abram, whose nephew Lot is still famous for incestuous lechery.

"Oh, the beautiful stories of the Old Testament. Yes, I was brought up on this shit. I was trained, I read it, I learned it, was taught to believe like everyone else in a world of conformists where the infidels are burned at the stake.

"But I am not an Abramist!" he cries out with passion. "I have chosen to be a member of an older tradition."

"Hear hear!" calls someone in the crowd.

And at this, Sage begins to sing. Hayden does not know the song, but many of the people around him do. Melissa joins the song with a lilting voice. The song's words are something about an Earth Goddess Mother and the seasons of the year. It all seems perfectly appropriate.

Hayden and Melissa talk late into the night, sitting around the fire. The conversation gradually works its way into very passionate, very erotic kissing, which soon moves to the sort of mutual-masturbation-through-the-clothes colloquially known as "heavy petting." This goes on for some time, and eventually moves to someone's tent, where with the application of other special techniques, some satisfaction is eventually obtained by them both, although they do not, as the vernacular would have it, "go all the way" at this time.

We'll leave them at that for now, and return to them the

next day as they wake up naked together and smile somewhat shyly .

"It's Beltane," she says.

"Happy Beltane," he says.

"Do you know what Beltane is?"

"Well, it's a Springtime ritual, isn't it? To celebrate the arrival of the flowers, and all that."

"The flowers are for fertility," she explains. "The Maypole is a giant phallus, and the act of placing the Maypole into a hole in the fertile soil of the Earth Mother represents the act of copulation, the source of all this fertility. And then to have all the beautiful young people of the community dancing around the Maypole, blessing it, tying ribbons around it... well, the implication is clear.

"The Springtime ritual always brings to mind the wildness of Pan," she continues. "Pan is the best-known personification of the archetype of The Horned God. These are nature gods, and the celebration of them is the celebration of the most basic sort of animal freedom, the sheer joy of living with wild abandon and divine inspiration: Kokopelli, Pan, Dionysus, the Horned God. To the Celts he had deer antlers, but it's basically the same concept. Abramist tradition associates goat-horned, cloven-hoofed Pan with evil, but that is because they associate sexuality with shame. We celebrate our sexuality, and call upon the phallic energy of The Horned God to bring us strength and vitality."

"Amen," he murmurs in assent, as she strokes his body gently with her fingertips.

"I want you to invoke the Horned God with me," she says in his ear.

"Okay," he breathes, moving closer to her.

"I want to feel your manly power inside of me," she says,

grabbing him.

"Yeah," he says, stroking her ass, moving a finger to her soft folds, so wet, slippery, open, inviting. He rubs her clit with a moistened finger. She kisses him wildly and throws him upon his back. Positioned over his throbbing erection, she leans forward, pressing her nipples against his chest, and says warmly into his ear, "I want you to get me pregnant."

His heart skips a beat as his brain thinks, "but I hardly know you..." Then she breathes on his neck and with a little kiss she sits up enough to look into his eyes, and smiles. He feels his excitement surge as he senses her so close.

She wants me to get her pregnant? he thinks. And he imagines himself spurting his semen, imagines her pregnant, with a baby inside her... To his surprise, he finds himself hugely turned on at the thought. Stiffer than ever, he moves up to touch her with it.

"Yeah," he says thickly. "Okay."

"Yeah?" she says back, excitedly. She sits down against him a bit. He can feel her, so wet, enveloping part of his shaft. He moves, she moves, riding him, sliding up and down, so good...

"Yeah," he says again. "Oh yeah."

She moves into that magical angle, and he penetrates her deeply.

"Ohhh," they both say.

"Yeah," she says.

"Uh-huh," he says.

"Oh," she says. "Oh yeah. Oh, oh yeah. Oh, like that, oh, yeah, yeah... yeah, oh, baby, oh yeah, oh yeah, oh yeah, oh, oh, oh, oh, aaaaaaaaaaaaaah!"

And he can't contain it any more, and he comes inside her as she orgasms around him, her whole body shuddering. Their first time together, and they come together. It seems so unlikely, and so perfect. He can't believe his good fortune.

Chapter III: Young Love

After his Beltane experience, our protagonist is brimming with confidence, smiling, strutting, even: standing tall, speaking louder in group settings. He even tells a joke. He thinks that perhaps it might be the first time he has told a joke in three – four? - years.

As for Melissa, well he really likes her. Due to his condition of paralytic insecurity, it takes him a couple days to summon the courage to call her; and then he gets her voicemail. When she doesn't call back, he tactfully waits a couple days, and calls her once more. Voicemail. He doesn't want to harass her if she doesn't want to talk to him. He would hate for her to think that he was acting like a stalker or something. So he doesn't try to call her again.

Well, he figures, *she must not have liked me, or maybe I said something stupid. Maybe she has a boyfriend she didn't tell me about. Who knows.*

Meanwhile, Melissa is over on her end of the phone, angry that he waited two days to call her. She thinks he's playing games. Then as if to prove her point, he only calls twice in four days, and gives up easily. *Well,* she figures, *he must not have liked me, or maybe he's just a player. He's just another guy who will say anything to get laid.*

It's a couple weeks after this, that her period doesn't start on the day she was expecting. *Well, could be the stress,* she thinks: *that's probably what makes my breasts hurt, too. They feel so swollen and tight.*

She tells herself this for most of a week; and then she goes down to the drugstore for a pregnancy test. Positive. Chance of false positive: slim. She gets another test, just in case: a different brand, from a different store. Still positive.

No doubt about who the father is. Even got his phone number somewhere in those "missed call" logs on her mobile. But right now she hates the bastard, and doesn't want to have anything to do with his sorry ass. He doesn't deserve her.

She continues to tell herself this for a few more weeks before she calls him up late one night. He can barely understand what she's saying; she sounds extremely upset.

"Are you all right?" he asks, concerned for her safety.

"I just need to talk to you," she says.

"Do you want to meet at the park?" he asks, thinking she would feel safer meeting him there, because he is still worried that she might think that he is a stalker.

So there they meet a short time later. The park is deserted, technically closed at this hour. They stroll beneath the majestic trees, among the brightly blooming flowers all bathed in the warm glow of the moonlight, beneath the billions and billions of stars.

"You remember when we invoked the gods at a fertility rite?" she asks.

"You mean, when we had unprotected sex at Beltane?"

"Sure, if you want to put it like that."

"Yeah, of course I remember. Did you, uh..."

"Well, it worked."

"Did it."

"Yeah."

"I see." (Pause.) "Well, I guess I kinda thought it might."

"Yeah?"

"Yeah." (Pause.) "It was really good sex."

She laughs a bit nervously. "Yeah, it was."

"So," he says. "Nine months from May first. What do you want to do about it?"

"Do about it?" She is worried, afraid that he is about to ask her to get an abortion.

Instead he says, "Well, I mean, do you want to move in together? I'm a bit of a slob but, you know, I'll do my best not to bug you."

"Okay," she giggles nervously.

"Because I think it will be easier to take care of the baby if we're living together."

"Definitely," she sighs.

"And, well," he says.

"Well?" she asks.

"Well, it would be best for the baby if its parents were in a stable, committed, long-term relationship."

"I think so too," she says.

"But, well, the thing is, I haven't really known you for very long."

She laughs. "Just a few weeks!"

"But you know, I really like you. I mean, I love you. Like, I love you as a person, and, uh, I really, um, already think of you as my girlfriend," he finishes in a small, embarrassed voice.

"I love you too," she says simply.

"So I guess, what I'm saying is, I hope you don't think it's, um, too soon? But, well, do you want to get married?"

"Yes," she says, and both their eyes fill with love and joy.

"Really?"

"Yes!" she laughs. "What, you don't believe me?"

"No I, I mean yeah but I, I thought you would take more convincing."

"You don't have to talk me into it.   I'm already convinced."

"That, that's great!" he says.

In the back of his mind, he is aware of reasonable objections to this turn of events. Statistics are against them. In an ideal world, they really should have gotten to know each other before conceiving; or at least dated for a couple weeks before the friggin' marriage proposal. But life is messy, and he is determined to make the best of what arrives. He keeps his secret misgivings to himself.

They kiss, and hold each other, there in the park, in the warm air of summertime, surrounded by blooming trees. Then they go back to her place.

"So," she tells him later, as they are lying on her rumpled bed, "conception at Beltane puts the baby's due date at Immolc, the Feast of Brigid."

"Which one is Immolc again?" he asks.

"Immolc is one of my favorite Sabbats," she says. "Brigid is an old Celtic goddess of springtime, fertility, the hearth fire and the more abstract fires of creativity and divine inspiration. Her feast day comes at the beginning of the lambing season. These days, Immolc rituals are not usually a big party for our local community. Maybe they will be someday. The Feast of Brigid was so important to ancient Pagans that the Abramists could not eliminate the holiday.   Instead, they had to appropriate it. They added a 'Saint Bridgette' to their Catholic pantheon. The goddess abides. She even came with her own predetermined feast day at the beginning of February, which the Abramists renamed 'Candlemas.'"

"I see," he says, wondering to himself if an institution with a pantheon can really be considered monotheistic.

"Oh, how fun!" she muses. "It will be our little Pagan baby: conceived at Beltane, and born at Immolc."

"Let's tell all our friends at the Summer Solstice!" he suggests.

"Litha," she fills in. "Yes, let's. That's a great idea. And we'll invite them to our handfasting at Lammas."

Chapter IV: Litha

It's only a few weeks later that the Pagan community all gets together to celebrate Litha, the Summer Solstice. The local group decides to return back to the forest camp where the community had celebrated Beltane. The long car trip gives Hayden plenty of time pursue some tangential line of thought and somehow prove beyond a shadow of a doubt that more than anything else, the Summer Solstice was an excellent reason to go camping.

Hayden shares a car with Nicholas and Melissa. Nicholas, as is his habit, launches into a dissertation at the first opportunity.

"The Summer Solstice," he says, "is the longest day of the year, and the shortest night. In our modern reckoning, Litha is the beginning of astronomical summer. In ancient times this was called 'midsummer.' It is one of the oldest and most universal of the Pagan holidays."

"But I've gone camping on the Summer Solstice before," Hayden objects, "long before I ever met up with you Pagan lot. It's just a great night to go camping, because it's the shortest night of the year."

"The Summer Solstice has been an important holiday tradition for people around the world, since long before recorded history," maintains Nicholas, ignoring the interruption.

"The Summer Solstice has a strong spiritual significance in many cultures throughout history," Melissa reminds them. "And I'm talking about people who could not have been in contact with each other: the Anasazi, the Druids, the Sinagua, the Babylonians, they all had summer solstice rites."

"Well," Nicholas adds, "and it's because the Summer Solstice is just naturally such an important marker in the year. It's a time of great hope, for an agricultural society: the crops are in the ground, and you're hoping like hell that the harvest will be good."

"And that may tie in with the tradition of wish-making at Litha," Melissa says.

"Yeah," Hayden muses, "Nicholas told me something about jumping over a bonfire?"

"It's fun," Melissa says. "But nobody really believes that stuff."

"Belief or not," says Hayden, "I think it sounds worth a try."

The night they arrive, it's a big party for everybody, and they have a fantastic time. Our protagonist plays a hand drum at the fire circle in the evening, and Melissa dances for him again, and this time he is not embarrassed to stare at her.

Later that night, after he and his intended have announced their plans to the community, as the evening darkens, Hayden gladly accepts several toasts of the mead horn. Then he makes a wish, takes a run, and hurls himself over the bonfire. Well, the fire isn't actually as big as it seems, and he ends up body slamming Sage on the far side. But Sage is generously forgiving about the incident, and they all have a good laugh.

On this night, the shortest night of the year, he and Melissa leave the main fire to sit out together. They talk through the night wrapped in blankets, leaning together in their camp chairs, resting their feet upon the huge old white weathered log, beaten free of bark by river rocks in seasonal floods; looking at the moon and the stars, kind of shivering a little bit, for as long as they can stand it, watching the darkly monochrome shadows of the trees become sharp grey silhouettes of trees and suddenly flame into brightly brilliant full-color glow before they retreat to the tent early in the cold morning, just as the birds begin their early chatter. It's a beautiful place, a beautiful night, a beautiful time of year, and he feels truly blessed to be able to share it all with such a beautiful woman.

The next morning they lounge outside their tent, drinking some camp coffee. The warm sunlight sparkles on the water of the nearby river; a cool breeze rustles the leaves of the trees, dappled and dancing with sunlight and shadow. It's just too damn perfect.

Hayden borrows somebody's old beater guitar that they've left laying around, and sings a really cheesy love song for Melissa. He's a bit embarrassed, because it feels so corny; but from the smile she gives him, it's clear that she thinks it's just about the sweetest thing she's ever heard.

Later that morning, they attend the main ritual. The community gathers round, those who haven't caroused beyond the point of no return. Dennis and Diana help everybody find a place in the circle. When everyone is in place, Sage stands in the center before them and begins the ceremony. She kindly explains what she is doing as she is doing it, for the benefit of the newcomers.

"There is no single accepted version of the Pagan ritual," she begins. "Different groups have their own traditions. Even within a given community, different individuals have their own preferred techniques for ritual practice. We are not a top-down organization where a paternalistic hierarchy dominates and dictates dogma. We are a truly grass-roots movement with everywhere different practices and observances, just as Pagans throughout the centuries have always had different ideas, rituals, and even different deities. Doubtless as time passes our ritual practices and traditions will continue to evolve, and blessed be. For now, this is my own personal preferred manner of invoking the higher powers.

"We cast the circle to create a sacred space," she tells them. "A sacred space is the place you are in when you are communing with that which is sacred in the world around you. A sacred space can be anywhere you make it. What it requires is a mindset: the sense that the present moment is outside the normal flow of daily life.

"To cast the circle, walk it, trace it, and invoke its protection. Then cast the quarters to align our spiritual selves with our physical reality, including the Earth's magnetic field and lei lines. We begin like the rising sun in the East, and from there we turn counter clockwise."

Then she intones the sacred words to cast the magic circle.

"We call upon the forces of the East: the element of the air, which symbolizes the intellect and the forces of the mind. Forces of the East, bless this circle with your presence. Hail, and welcome."

"Hail, and welcome," echoes the group.

Some birds twitter from the nearby trees.

"We call upon the forces of the South: the element of fire, the Sun with its bright blazing energy, and the passions of sex and even war. Forces of the South, bless this circle with your presence. Hail, and welcome."

"Hail, and welcome," the group replies.

The birds flutter off noisily.

"We call upon the forces of the West: the element of water, the life-sustaining essence, which symbolizes emotion and romantic love. Forces of the West, bless this circle with your presence. Hail, and welcome."

"Hail, and welcome."

"We call upon the forces of the North: the element of the earth, the source of all, the foundation, the giver, the goddess. Forces of the North, bless this circle with your presence. Hail, and welcome."

"Hail, and welcome."

Then she begins to chant:

"This time is not a time. This place is not a place. This time is not a time. This place is not a place."

And the group echoes back to her, "This time is not a time. This place is not a place."

"Now we exist between the worlds," says Sage. "As above, so below."

There is a pause. Hayden looks around uncertainly. Some people have their eyes closed; many look intently serious.

"Now," says Sage, "everybody can go ahead and sit down for this next part. Are you comfortable? All right, well get comfortable, now, and relax. Good."

And she leads them on a guided meditation, raising energy and focusing power. At first Hayden finds himself feeling sort of silly about participating in something that maybe seems a little bit New Age; but then he remembers that the Buddhist monks who practice meditation also have more robust Alpha wave patterns in their EEGs. Based on this, he decides that the present exercise, if akin to meditation, would be at the worst harmless.

"Raising energy is usually more efficient in a group setting," Sage explains. "However, one who is in touch with their spirit need not be dependent on the group. An individual can create a sacred space and raise energy at any time, by invoking a harmonious state of mind. The ability to do this bestows grace, fortitude, courage, tolerance, and patience; and these, in turn, foster good will. Paths open themselves to one who displays these qualities."

The exercise only goes on for twenty, maybe thirty minutes. This isn't to be a test of their endurance, like a fiery sermon oratory. After the guided meditation and the explanation, they sit in silence for a moment to reflect on the experience. Then they stand up, and Sage concludes the ritual.

"Spirits of the East, we thank you. Be well, stay if you will, go if you must. Hail, and farewell."

"Hail, and farewell," the group echoes back.

"Spirits of the South, we thank you. Be well, stay if you will, go if you must. Hail, and farewell."

"Hail, and farewell."

"Spirits of the West, we thank you. Be well, stay if you will, go if you must. Hail, and farewell."

"Hail, and farewell."

"Spirits of the North, we thank you. Be well, stay if you will, go if you must. Hail, and farewell."

"Hail, and farewell."

"And all you, beautiful people, members of our spiritual communities, friends, sisters, and brothers, we thank you. Be well, stay if you will, go if you must, but go in peace. The circle is open but unbroken. Blessed be."

"Blessed be," some of them echo back.

"So mote it be," she says.

"So mote it be," they all echo back.

"So mote it be!" she repeats, louder.

"So mote it be!" they all cry out in response. A wave of

feeling joins them in joy as the Summer Solstice sun sends its radiance shining all around. The circle breaks up in a jubilant mood, and as small groups scatter, Pagans go dancing down forest paths.

Chapter V: Lammas

By Lammas, the weather is starting to get hot and dry. The clothes on the girls grow skimpier, and life is good. The year's harvest is beginning to ripen in the fields. A quick stop at a roadside blackberry patch yields a few handfuls; some slightly sour, others bursting with ripe sweetness.

A smaller group of Hayden and Melissa's close friends gather at a verdant wilderness location for the handfasting ceremony. Everyone comes prepared to have a grand old time.

An altar is built and covered with flowers. The circle is cast; the directions of the compass are invoked.

"My friends," says Sage, "we welcome you all here today. This is both a handfasting and a legal wedding ceremony. You are all witnesses, and we are pleased that you could be here to rejoice with us. This woman," she continues, indicating Melissa, "is one of my favorite people in the whole world. She is just a sparkling joy to be around, a shining star wherever she goes." Turning to Hayden, Sage tells the group, "And I've only known this young man for a few months. But what I know about him is that he makes my friend happy, and that's enough for me. She is simply the happiest I've ever seen her. Look at her, she's glowing!" They all look at Melissa, who is radiant and beautiful next to her man. "And if you make each other that happy, then my blessings be upon you both.

"Now, your life together won't always be easy," Sage the

Spiritual Leader continues. "Your life together will present many challenges. Life always puts obstacles in our way. It is the way of life. But if you put your trust in each other, be each other's strength, then you will get past every difficulty, and nothing will be insurmountable." She pauses. She looks at them both. "So."

She turns to Melissa.

"Do you?"

"I do," Melissa says.

Then to Hayden, "Do you?"

"I do," he says.

"Then I hereby pronounce you handfasted in the sight of our community, and legally married under the laws of our great State. So mote it be. Now, this is the only time when everyone actually wants to see you kiss. Go for it."

And they do.

That night, in their tent:

"Oh, my wife," he says.

"Oh, my husband," she says.

"Oh, yes," they both say. "Oh, yes!"

Their honeymoon is a four-day weekend of camping in the woods. They bathe in the river, they cook over a fire, they sleep under the stars.

Meanwhile, the rest of the local Pagan community joins them at the campground for a big Lammas celebration.

So the day after the wedding, the wedding party is joined by even more members of the larger Pagan community, and they're all out having a proper Lammas ritual. Sage has cast the circle and intoned the cardinal directions to create a ritual space. She begins to discuss the Pagan tradition of Lammas.

"Lammas," she says, "is a cross-quarter day. Today is the midpoint between the Summer Solstice and the Autumnal

Equinox. Historically, Lunasa was the feast of Lugh[2], the hero god of many talents. In ancient times this festival continued for an entire month, and Lunasa was the name of that month. This is a time of joy and plenty. The sun is warm, the harvest is ripening, and we can rejoice that we are among friends."

Then suddenly, without warning, Sage's introduction is interrupted as the camp is attacked by two truckloads full of violent local Abramists.

The attackers drive in to the campground loudly, shooting guns in the air, engines revving, tires squealing, country music blaring, kicking up clouds of dust. They chase people with their trucks. Worried mothers snatch their small children from the wheels of death.

The attackers proceed to trash the campsite, driving right over people's tents and belongings with the tractor tires on their jacked-up trucks, destroying expensive camping gear, and completely crushing the group's beautiful, time-consuming decorations. They smash the Maypole with a pickup truck, and drive right through the fire pit (which is not lit, since it is just mid-day) scattering the stones of the fire ring.

The local men lean out the truck windows, spitting chaw from stained lips, waving their firearms and shouting insults at the Pagans, who are telling them to go away.

A sneering passenger in one vehicle shouts at Melissa, with his face contorted by the angry righteousness of hatred, "Let's see your titties, you fuckin' slut!"

The other vehicle has stopped in the center of the campground, and Dennis is shouting at the driver. Standing bravely near the driver's side window, he says, "This is a

---

2   Lugh is pronounced "Loo"

private function. We have reserved this space. You're disturbing the peace, you're threatening our safety, you're destroying our property. You're not welcome here when you behave like this. You should leave now."

"Fuck you, devil worshipper!" shouts the driver. "This park is in our county, and you drugged-out hippies are the ones who aren't welcome here. So take your Satanism, and fuck off!" At this, the driver floors the gas on his truck and veers left in an attempt to sideswipe Dennis. The truck does not strike Dennis, but it comes so close to Sage, who is standing near him, that she is forced to back away precipitously. She trips over a rock, or perhaps a piece of charred firewood from the scattered fire pit; and she falls painfully, crying out, grasping her sprained her ankle as she writhes on the dusty ground.

"Ugly old hag!" shouts the other truck's passenger at Sage as she lies on the ground cringing in pain.

The trucks drive back out of the park, the occupants screaming unintelligible insults, shooting a few more rounds from their guns and revving their engines as they drive away.

As this is going on, Hayden runs for his notebook. As the trucks are screaming out of the park, he surreptitiously chases after them, keeping low behind some shrubs; and he is able to get close enough to read their license plates, which he writes down in his notebook.

But when Dennis goes down to the local police station to file a complaint, he is totally brushed off.

"Well, what did they actually do?" asks the deputy, declining to examine the license plates in Hayden's notebook. "They drove through the campground?"

"Shouting insults and shooting guns the whole time," answers Dennis heatedly.

"Well, I'm sure you had some choice words for them; and shooting guns is not against the law. So what's the actual problem? What are you asking me to charge them with? Did they break anything?"

"Yes! They smashed my friend's tent and camping chairs with their truck; and they totally destroyed our decorations that cost a lot of money and took a lot of time to make."

"Decorations?"

"Streamers," says Dennis.

"The Mayple," says Diana.

"Bunches of flowers," says Melissa.

"A *papier-mâché* bust of the Goddess," says Sage.

"Costume butterfly wings," says Hayden.

"And they drove right through our fire pit," concludes Phoenix.

The official response is not empathetic. "The park is public property," argues the deputy. "You shouldn't have been setting up your decorations and camping gear where they obstructed a roadway. I should write you a ticket."

"It was in a campsite!" Dennis maintains.

"I'm still not hearing anything very serious. Did anyone get hurt?"

"Yes! They nearly hit a 60-year-old woman with their truck! She sprained her ankle trying to get out of the way!"

"Wait, but you say they didn't actually hit her? I can't go charging them with a crime just because some old woman fell down. If she's so feeble and frail, then what's she doing camping out in the wilderness?"

"What? Are you serious?" asks Dennis incredulously.

"Yup. This whole thing sounds like a big misunderstandin'."

"They sexually harassed me," says Melissa.

"Well, that's your word against theirs, ain't it, sweetheart?" says the officer, eyeing her up and down. Returning his attention to Dennis he says, "Look, just coz you disagree with someone, don't mean a crime's been committed. The way I heard it, there was a lot of illegal drug use out at that event. I suggest, if you don't want us to start scrutinizing your belongings, you skeedaddle on out of town and stop provoking the citizens with your Wikkedness."

"You mean Wicca?"

"Whatever you call it. Sounds like devil-worshipping to me. Oughta be a law against it."

"Actually, there's this little law they call the First Amendment, that protects our right to - "

"Don't even start with me on the Constitutional stuff, boy. I think we're done here."

And he gets up and walks away.

"Now we know," Phoenix says in the parking lot outside the police station. "There is no official recourse, and no protection."

"Then do we take matters into our own hands?" asks Hayden.

"And do what?" objects Sage. "Exact retribution? I think the police would be sure to prosecute *us*."

"But we have to protect ourselves," says Phoenix.

"Well, we're leaving now," says Sage.

"And when we come back next year?" returns Phoenix.

"Oh, by then, we'll be ready," says Dennis. Sage gives him a look, but the thought has been spoken.

Of course, many community members have already privately decided not to return the next year, as a direct consequence of this unpleasantness with the locals. But there's always turnover in these types of groups and organizations and events; and next year is a long way off.

*   *   *

Now that Melissa has moved in, Hayden is busier in the evenings after work. Family life means cooking real meals, having real conversations, and occasionally doing some real cleaning, too. Plus, the place is a bit small. They both have a bunch of stuff, so there's sorting and packing that must be done as well. Some of the overflow is deposited in storage. And in the midst of all the chaos, the young couple is bathed in a joyful excitement at feeling the baby's first movements within Melissa's belly.

Hayden doesn't have a lot of free time. But for the next couple weeks, every time he has the opportunity, he writes letters to the press. He finds the address of every local newspaper and blog in a fifty mile radius. He sends them messages in which he describes the incident. He provides a detailed account of the threats, the destruction of property, and the way his pregnant wife was verbally assaulted on their honeymoon weekend. He describes the refusal of the police to look into their complaint. He sends each letter off, confident that it will spark indignation on behalf of a persecuted religious minority.

He gets no response. The letters are not published. The press ignores them. Nobody cares.

Chapter VI: Mabon

They are lucky this year, for Mabon enjoys the last of the waning summer warmth, even as autumn has clearly begun. The leaves have been turning colors and falling from the trees for weeks already. The first rains of the seasons have washed away the summer heat, and there is a faint note of damp chill in the night air.

The midday sun cheers them on their way to the festivities, while Nicholas explains the history of the modern Pagan name for the Autumnal Equinox.

"Mabon," he says, "was a Celtic deity who the Roman soldiers believed was an aspect of their god Apollo. So he had the attributes of being a sun god, with qualities of healing, hunting, poetry & music, and of course love, which is important in youth. Mabon[3] was the youthful god, the Son of Modron the Mother Goddess, and he was an expert hunter. For people who live off the land, the ability to catch your dinner is an important skill, so Mabon earned his place in the Welsh mythology. He figures most notably in the Bardic epic, the Mabinogion, which relates how he was kidnapped as an infant, rescued by King Arthur's Knights, and how he then helped to hunt a magic boar.

---

3   The name "Mabon" is pronounced with the emphasis on the first
     syllable, with a nasal "a" sound as in "bat." The "o" is almost silent.

"The Druids use a different name for the harvest feast at the Autumnal Equinox; but the ancient words are difficult to pronounce[4]. That's why many modern Pagans have accepted the convention suggested by Aidan Kelly, to name this holy day after the youthful god, Mabon."

In order to get together for the Mabon holiday, the group rents cabins high in the mountains. The craggy summits and vast distances are an impressive and splendid spectacle, and Hayden loves the mountains. At the same time, he finds himself wondering why he always has to drive so far away to hang out with people who live nearby.

Once the group is together, it's natural that some of them want to discuss the incident that occurred on Lammas. Their community has come under attack; no resolution is forthcoming from official channels; and the group is collectively feeling persecuted. Now they need to talk through the issues in order to reach some catharsis.

The group is sitting in a circle around the fire that evening when Phoenix finds that he can contain his sentiments no longer, and he must share them with the group or he will explode. Off on one side, some people are playing drums. The others are talking amongst themselves, snacking and passing the mead horn. Not content to merely address himself to his neighbor, Phoenix leaps up to address the group with his characteristic liveliness. One conversation moves away, and the rest grow quieter as he begins his rant.

"Normally," he says, "Mabon is a time of peaceful reflection. The Autumnal Equinox signifies that the time to prepare for winter is upon us; but it is also a time to enjoy the bounty of the harvest, and give thanks for what has been

---

4   *Meán Fómhair* or *Alban Elfed*

received.

"On the Equinox itself, the day and the night are the same length. We can meditate upon the balance of natural forces, and prepare ourselves spiritually for the long nights which we know lie ahead. This spiritual preparation is important; for just as we must store up food to eat and fuel to eat our homes, so we must store up spiritual energies to keep our hearts warm through the long cold winter nights ahead. That is normally what I would be meditating on, this evening. I would want to talk with you all about The Balance of All Things."

Phoenix looks around, notes the group's inattentiveness, and forges ahead. "But I have a confession to make, my brothers and sisters!" he cries out with feeling. "I do not feel balanced! I feel threatened. I feel like our community is under attack for our beliefs, and there is no protection to be had from official channels. The only solution is to go on the offensive. But which path to take? I open the floor to debate."

Some members of the group, including our protagonist, favor retaliation by any means necessary. Dark Marc speaks for them. "Adopt the attackers' tactics in self-defense," he calls out. "In fact, we're justified if we escalate the confrontation at the slightest provocation."

"We are not safe from our enemies under the present circumstances," agrees Phoenix. "We must strike back. They destroyed our property, they shot guns at us, they tried to hit us with their trucks, they harassed us. They have threatened our families and our very lives!" he roars. "They pose an existential threat. I call upon the gods of war, Ares, Thor, and Odin, to bless our coven with courage and fortitude as we strike back in defense of our lives, our community, and our Constitutional rights."

"You just hold on a minute there, " objects Sage in a firm,

clear voice. "Answering violence with violence is not the path to peace. Heaping wrong upon wrong will not bring about reconciliation. Rather than lash out at those who have wronged us, we must try to build understanding and trust between our communities. We must foster good will and spread our love of all that is beautiful in the world. Then the larger community will unite behind us, and we will earn protection and recompense for our losses."

"We don't have to ask for our fundamental rights," Phoenix vents. "Why should we have to get down on our knees and beg and plead with an uncaring society to please let us exist, to please allow us to retain our lives, our liberty, and our property? I shall ask no man's permission! I exist! Here I stand, and he who threatens me shall be rewarded with my fist in his face!"

"What are you going to do, shoot some redneck to make a point? That will be great public relations for our community. The Abramists will parade you out for a show trial and some vindictive local judge will throw the book at you. National talk shows and forums will be filled with Abramist propaganda about murderous Pagans who go around shooting hometown heroes. There may even be a crackdown as a result, the FBI will classify us as a terrorist organization and we'll all have to go into hiding as they slowly round us all up..."

"That is the very definition of a totalitarian state!" roars Phoenix. "If I am jailed for defending myself, that is injustice; but if my entire community is persecuted for an action that I myself undertook alone, then that is a blatant case of communal retribution against a civilian population, which is expressly prohibited by the Geneva Conventions. Under those circumstances, according to John Locke's fundamental precepts of government, I would be not merely justified but materially obligated to take up arms against the State."

"What is it with you and taking up arms all of a sudden? You don't even own a gun."

"It's time I should go get one."

"Hush, now. That's enough of that. I understand that you're angry, we all are, but this isn't helping. We don't need to go around shooting anyone or inciting a revolution. What's required is not to kill our enemies, but to convert them. We must follow the model of the Abramist missionaries, and actively work to convert the entire world to our way of thought."

"What, are you envisioning youths in suits and ties, going door to door, saying, 'Hi, have you accepted Gaia the Earth Goddess as your path to love and happiness in this life?'"

"Yes, if it's necessary, that's a great idea. What's more, we must improve upon the missionary model, by adopting more modern methods of preaching the Word of the Goddess. In the Internet era, it's no longer necessary to convert people one individual at a time by speaking to them in person. A single popular blog post or YouTube video might reach millions."

Phoenix falls back with a shrug and takes a seat as Sage goes on.

"All we have to do is plant the seed," she says. "There are millions of people who are only marginally attached to Abramist faiths. If they see an opportunity to connect to something deeper, they may well come over to our side.

"Let them know that they can join us and still keep their important traditions and holidays. We don't believe the 'one god' fallacy. As far as we're concerned, you can be a Pagan and a Christian too; if you want to, it doesn't bother us. Why, the Irish have done it for centuries!"

"As have the Mexicans," interjects Phoenix from his seat.

"Indeed. Most of South America worships The Goddess and performs Pagan rites handed down from their ancestors; they merely cloak their rituals in Christianity and the cult of Mary for the sake of the form.

"We must demonstrate to the marginally attached Abramists that Paganism is more fun, more relevant to their lives and beliefs, and fully compatible with their existing family traditions. If we can do this, then we will begin to convert some of them. Even if we don't win their allegiance, as long as we win their sympathy, a respect and tolerance, then we will have won. Convince the Unitarians that they have really been Pagans all along..."

"Actually," speaks up Dylan, "there is already a branch of the Unitarian Church that is specifically Pagan in its beliefs and practices. It's on the Internet."

"There, see? We just need to get in contact to enlist their help and support. We just need to join forces.

"Next, we go to work on the agnostics and the atheists. Explain to the agnostics that Paganism is the answer: it provides total flexibility of belief, an infinite pantheon of gods and spirits for every occasion, and core values based on respect for the Earth Mother and for each other. There is no written doctrine or fixed theology. It's all about the individual path to spiritual transcendence in the context of communing with nature, sometimes in a group setting.

"Explain to the atheists and intellectuals that the Pagan gods are symbols, archetypes, representations of an aspect of nature or the human condition. Mystical beings may be thought of as stand-ins for human psychology and natural forces. It turns out that the highest gods of all are the laws of physics, gravity, and the strong nuclear binding force that constrains the protons in atomic nuclei against electromagnetic repulsion." She paused for breath. "As long as you think of mythology as a symbol, Paganism is fully compatible with the laws of science. In fact, Paganism is the only modern religion that directly celebrates the revolutions of the Earth around the Sun, the Moon around the Earth, and the stars around the cosmos.

"And finally, be sure to capture the interest of the youth. Demonstrate that Paganism is sexy, and provides a great excuse to throw a happenin' party. Show them pictures of beautiful young Pagans dancing the Maypole and having a great time."

"Tell them about the Tantric Temple," says Melissa.

"Do you really think they want to hear that?" Marc promptly retorts.

"I think it's the best part," she returns, standing her ground.

Sage continues. "Once you begin to make inroads with the youth on a large scale, then you finally gain some proper recognition from the media; and once they go from ignoring you to noticing you, their attention can become something of an onslaught."

Sensing a brief lull, Phoenix stands back up. "Somebody made a good point," he says, "when they brought up the Pagan Unitarians. In fact, there are a lot of these various Pagan groups, doing their own thing, all over the country, around the world. The majority of us may be Wiccans, for now, but there are a lot of quasi-Wiccan Pagans with divergent views and practices.

"If we could somehow combine our forces, we would be stronger. Agree to a charter that prohibits dogma and respects the diversity of our views and practices. The purpose of organizing is not to dictate the belief or actions of the members. The purpose is to present a unified face to the world, and represent ourselves from a position of strength.

"We need to talk about what we have in common, not how we differ. There's presently very little communication between all these different groups, or between independent practitioners, and I think it would give us a sense of pride if we could have some idea about how many of us there really are.

"And we need to talk to similar groups as well. In Britain, there are many adherents to Druidism and The Ancient Order of Bards. I would love to join forces with these guys. I would love to reach out to the postmodernist adherents of Jediism, and tell them that we truly, deeply believe that the Force is with us all."

"And there's no such thing as mitichlorians!" shouts Hayden, to general snickering from the group.

"Let the Buddhists, the Taoists, and the Zoroastrians know that our philosophy is fully compatible with theirs. In fact, the more liberal Hindus effectively share our belief system already."

"And the Cult of Kali has an international following," says Melissa.

"Can I say something?" asks Diana.

"Of course," says Sage, and yields the floor.

"Uh, yeah, you know, I totally agree with what Sage has been saying. But I just wanted to say, as we go about this, we must not allow ourselves to be fooled into thinking that all this will magically happen all by itself. Real magic takes real work. If we want the magic to happen, then we have to make it happen. We can pray, raise energy, meditate, chant incantations, and cast spells, if we are so inclined. But if that's all we do, then nothing will get done. We should also borrow tactics from the major corporations. We should engage in commercial activities on behalf of our cause, the way a political campaign would. We should have a fundraising arm, and a marketing arm, and a public relations arm. We need to formulate our message, make it accessible, get it out there, and make it known."

"You're saying, what, that we should start a business?" says Marc.

"Sure. Why not? We can sell Pagan calendars to raise money for our public relations activities. We can sell handcrafted goods, hand-sewn clothing, wreaths and garlands, silk-screened T-shirts, books of incantations and spells, and books about the history and practice of the various branches of Paganism. Better yet, we can conduct surveys and find out what people want to buy, and how much they might be willing to pay for it. We don't even have to rely on volunteers. We'll pay the people who produce the goods, or sell their creations on commission. We'll increase the wealth of the community, and we'll use the profits to pay for our publicity. We'll buy advertisements, and hold large events. We will stage rallies with speakers, concerts, happenings, all to raise awareness, and spread our message."

Hayden is so caught up by Diana's enthusiasm that he is just about to let out a great cheer when Marc speaks up again.

"Yeah, but what about all this is new?" he says. "There are plenty of websites that sell handcrafted crap, and nobody's getting rich there. Besides, Pagans have been trying to spread the word for years. We've been having festivals and rituals to honor the Sabbats, the Solstices and Equinoxes, and yet here we are, with no place of our own, camping and renting Grange halls. There are plenty of people trying to spread the word. There are a ton of Pagan websites on the Internet."

"There are a ton of Pagan websites, yes," Diana retorts,

"but have you noticed that they all *suck?* Don't get me wrong, there is some great content out there, but true believers are not necessarily great designers. A plethora of homemade-looking, unprofessional, Do-It-Yourself websites will not carry nearly as much weight with the public as one or two high-quality, professionally designed websites with high-quality interactive messaging features, and comments closely administered to prevent them filling up with spam. A professional site will cost real money, but buying advertising will cost even more, and we just have to budget for all of that, plus our other marketing activities."

Diana pauses and looks around.

"We can raise the money," she concludes. "We can make this work. We can do it. I have faith. But it will require us to get organized."

Chapter VII: Sowan

By Sowan, the weather is decidedly damp; although the neighborhood children are thrilled that the rain lets up long enough for them to go Trick or Treating.

Needless to say, the group has not magically become organized overnight. Even the events of the Lammas Attack have not been sufficient to motivate people to attend meetings, and set agendas, and form committees, and draw up plans, and raise money, and all the rest. It is a very small community, this local group of Pagan friends, and in the face of institutionalized powerlessness, they growl and snarl and then go back to their lives.

That is to say, most of them do. Hayden remains really angry that his wedding honeymoon was disturbed, and that his wife was insulted. He feels personally attacked, and he isn't going to stand for it.

After conferring with Melissa, he calls Diana, who speaks to him for a while, then hands the phone over to Dennis, who does not dwell on pleasantries.

"When do you want to meet?" Dennis says.

"I don't know, how about this Saturn Day?"

"Perfect. Let's say two o'clock. What's the location?"

"I don't have a..."

"We can meet at my place, there should be plenty of room. Who's coming?"

"Um, us? I mean there's me, and my wife here, and you, and..."

"Right, and probably a few friends, let's say probably six people, maybe eight at the outside. Sounds good. See you then."

"Okay! Thanks!"

"Yup. All right then." [click.]

This brusque exchange begins a tradition of weekly Saturn Day meetings at Diana's house. It is a modest home, but Dennis is a craftsman, and his meticulous renovations are inspirational improvements.

Out in the small back yard is a rock garden with a bird bath and some kind of small plant. It's nothing spectacular; but it's peaceful. The peacefulness of the rock garden permeates the entire atmosphere at the house. Hayden sometimes feels almost as if he would happily go over to Dennis and Diana's house just to hang out with the rocks in the back yard.

The meetings usually consist of the four of them plus Nicholas and his flavor of the week girlfriend. Sometimes Phoenix shows up, and on those days, less work gets done, although everyone has an enjoyable time. Occasionally Sage and a small retinue stop by for fifteen minutes or three hours.

On the first of these events, in celebration of Sowan, a few of the group members decide to put on a ritual performance of an ancient story about the end of summer.   They dress in costumes and assume roles as they perform a reenactment of the myth of Demeter and Persephone. Diana plays Demeter; her teenage daughter plays Persephone; Dennis plays Pluto; and Nicholas plays Hermes. The ritual reenactment reminds everyone about the deeper meanings of the ancient Pagan traditions, which tie us to the circle of life and the wheel of the year.

After Sowan, the group begins meeting every Saturn Day. Most of the rest of the group's meetings tend to be more practical. The discussions range wide, but the small group's members feel that they have a shared purpose that brings them together, weekend after weekend.

On the second weekend, as they are discussing their plans, Sage addresses the gathering about their direction and purpose.

"Our mission," she says, "is to let it be known, constantly, in small ways, here and there, that the old ways are not forgotten; that the old gods are still honored; that the old traditions continue to be practiced in new ways. We demand the respect we deserve, as practitioners of the Old Ways: to have our beliefs recognized as being just as valid as the beliefs of any Abramist sect."

"Well that's an interesting point," says Marc. "Right now, we're an upstart community of poorly organized and oft-bickering clans. Some of us meet to observe the Sabbats; others may even get together more often, for a while, at those times in our lives when we're not otherwise occupied. But even the most organized of us don't have anything like the resources of even a small community church."

"Maybe the Unitarians," adds Dylan, humorously.

"Not even close to the Unitarians," Marc retorts with fire. "None of us are as organized or well-funded as any of the more mainstream religious groups."

He pauses for effect and continues loudly, "But imagine if we won. What would happen if we un-seated the power of the Abramists as we dream? Wouldn't we then become the establishment? Wouldn't we eventually come to embody everything that we are now fighting against?"

Phoenix takes up the challenge. "You're suggesting," he says, "imagine some hypothetical future in which the Pagans are as well-established as the Abramists are now. Would we not then be as they are? Verily, I think you have it right. Once a religious institution becomes backed by the force of a civil establishment, then it automatically becomes tyrannical, regardless of the philosophy of its founding premise.

"But," he continues, "our objective is not to seize power for our sect. The purpose is not to attempt to become the establishment. The purpose is to return power from the establishment to the people. Because we are not organized, our practice of our faith is a disorganized, highly localized, deeply personal and fiercely individualistic practice. The experience is unique from tribe to tribe, much as spiritual practices have evolved in unique flavors from tribe to tribe throughout the eons.

"When we participate in our rituals, we join in a group activity, which is a way of raising energy; but we are communing with the forces of nature in a tradition that is older than Abramism, older than any other living religion, older even than humanity itself; and that tradition and these forces of nature raise their own energy.

"The point is that our spirituality is a spirituality of the individual. We don't imagine ourselves becoming the dominant force in the world, because we don't approach spirituality as a means of telling other people what to do.

"Some of us, just a few of us, are beginning to imagine ourselves working behind the scenes to cause the world's dominant powers to lose some of that power.

"We seek a redistribution of power. We are the Robin Hood of control, we seek to take it away from the powerful and return it to the powerless. Oh, but that is what they fear most, more than thieves; for Robin Hood can be hunted down by the Sheriff of Nottingham, and the rich nobles he stole from, they can always get more money by exploiting the peasants; but once Robin Hood inspires the people to ask why the nobles are rich, and why the Church can afford such splendidly expensive cathedrals, while the poor hovel in filth; then these questions become ideas, and ideas can spread faster than plague, and suddenly the masses wake up.

"We want to return power to the individual. The purpose is not to assume the position presently held by the establishment. This isn't about executing the Czar only to become Josef Stalin. This is about lifting the clouds that have obscured our humanity for the last two thousand years of Abramist supremacy, and bringing out some sunshine to light the way and shine the light to illuminate the future of civilization."

"And how will we do that then?" challenges Marc.

"Well, right now we're planning a guerrilla art installation," mentions Sage.

"Gorilla art?" queries Dylan.

"Flower petals," explains Melissa, "glued to the side of a building with egg whites to make a picture of the Goddess Mother and the rebirth of the Sun."

"How are you going to show that?" asks Hayden.

She just smiles. "You'll have to wait and see. You'll love it. Right now we have to pre-sort all the different color petals into bins, to speed up the process, when we're on site during the operation."

Diana pipes up then, and brashly describes the planned work of art. It is to be a rabbit-headed woman on her back, legs spread, giving vaginal birth to a solar ball, with the caption, "The Rebirth of the Sun," for any who might have missed the subtlety of the pictorial reference.

"The point is to wake the people up," says Sage, "to let

them know that we are here, to make a statement that our gods are older than yours and you can hunt us down but you can't wipe out our way of thought."

"I just don't see that this type of action would make an impact on the scale we're talking about," objects Marc.

"But hundreds of such actions..." begins Diana.

"Would take a lot of time and volunteers," Marc cuts her off.

"You know," says Hayden, "it would be faster to adopt modern marketing methods. Buy a mailing list, do a print run, and send a postcard to every household in a select set of zip codes; specially chosen so that if you were to plot all the zip codes that received post cards on a map of the United States, the result would look like a gigantic Wiccan pentagram; a bit lopsided, to be sure, but nonetheless, the intent is unmistakable."

He continues brainstorming out loud. "The postcards say on the front in huge letters, 'May your life be blessed with fertility and prosperity this Ostara.' And there's a friendly picture of an Easter egg with a star dyed on it. But the back of the card says,

"Easter is a Pagan ritual honoring Eostar, goddess of fertility. We celebrate life at the time of the Vernal Equinox, to rejoice for the rebirth of the sun, the return of Persephone from Hades, and give voice to our hopes for an auspicious spring planting. This Ostara, remember the ancient meanings of rabbits and eggs. May the Goddess bless you with prosperity in the seasons to come."

Marc is beginning to get angry. "Are you serious? Printing and mailing that many postcards would cost tens of thousands of dollars. Easily. Maybe hundreds of thousands. I don't know. It would be tremendously, fabulously expensive."

"That's not a big expenditure, for a large corporation."

"But we're not a large corporation."

"Well, we could form one. Better yet, a non-profit. We'll be a church!"

"Weren't we just discussing the dangers of becoming the establishment?" Marc prods.

"I really don't see it as a risk," Hayden maintains.

"Well, I call for other voices. What does the group think?"

"Actually, I'm glad you asked," Diana speaks up. "Because this whole discussion sounds real similar to something I was saying back at Mabon. What we require is to get organized: formally, and with a purpose. If that means establishing a legal framework for our organization, then I am all in favor of doing so, because I truly believe that it will be the most efficient and successful way to proceed. And whether we file the paperwork to register as a limited liability company, or a nonprofit corporation, or a licensed charity, or an actual church, or the bloody second coming of the Merovingian Dynasty, well it's all the same to me, so long as we quit sitting here jabbering about it, and go do this shit."

Hayden is quite surprised to hear Diana speak in this manner; but he finds himself enthusiastically applauding her speech.

Chapter VIII: Pagans, Incorporated

The very next Moon Day, Dennis and Diana file the necessary paperwork to form and register a nonprofit corporation.

Quiet, reliable Dennis is a natural manager. He takes care of details. He does not ask for advice, nor does he receive it kindly. He simply observes, recognizes needs, and takes steps to eliminate problems. He is the man who gets things done. He makes the group's activities flow smoothly.

Energetic, gregarious Diana is a natural leader. People follow her without being asked, because they instinctively want to be around her, want to please her. She too recognizes needs; she also recognizes talents, and is able to delegate tasks accordingly.

Inspired by this definitive direction, on the third weekend, the group discusses how to raise money.

"We need money," Diana states, opening the discussion. "How are we going to get money? We can't steal it, we'd go to jail. We could pray for it; but that's not likely to help much."

"We need something to sell," Hayden agrees. "Even as a nonprofit, the core of the business model is revenue generation. We could ask for donations, but the reality is that very few, if any, of our friends in the Pagan community would be able to donate large amounts of cash. But some of the same people who can't afford to give their money away, might be more than willing to donate their time and their labor."

Those present respond with a variety of ideas.

"Yeah, members of the broader Pagan community could contribute hand-crafted products and service offerings," says Phoenix.

"We could sell baby clothes, cloth diapers and slings," says Diana.

"Original paintings, postcards and prints," suggests Nicholas.

"Or how about floral arrangements for weddings and special events," says Sage.

"Potholders, placemats and rugs," offers Dylan.

"Plenty of adult novelty costumery: fairy wings, fantasy horns, capes, cloaks, and masks," says Marc.

"Don't forget the sexy leather outfits," says Melissa, whose visibly pregnant body is innately sexy in its quintessential fecundity, a beauty with no need of trappings or enhancements.

"We'll need a website," says Hayden, always down to business. "Maybe even a couple of websites: one for the central organization, and one for each of those primary product lines. I'll help you set them up."

"Better yet," says Phoenix, "we should sell a line of Pagan Calendars. The calendars mark the phases of the Moon, note all the Solstices and Equinoxes, and give the Pagan names for all the major holidays."

"I love it," says Nicholas. "At the top, the Pagan Calendar prints both names for the days of the week. So the English names would be on the top line in large bold letters: Sun Day, Moon Day, Tyr's Day, Odin's Day, Thor's Day, Freya Day, Saturn Day.

"Below that in smaller italics it would have the Roman names: Sun Day, Moon Day, Mars Day, Mercury Day, Jupiter

Day, Venus Day, Saturn Day."

"You know," mentions Melissa aside to Hayden, "the original Saturn Day, or Saturnalia, is said to have been quite a feast. It was celebrated annually, at the time of the Winter Solstice, and appears to have been, ah, *penetrated* with orgiastic overtones."

"But how would a calendar like that work in our modern society?" objects Dennis, being practical. "It wouldn't even say Wednesday at all."

"It doesn't need to," soothes Diana. "It says Odin's Day, and below that, it says Mercury Day in italics. It's the central day of the week, appearing in its usual place. I think people will figure it out. After all, this is supposed to be a Pagan calendar."

So they decide to go with the traditional Pagan names for the days of the week, and omit the modern variants from the calendar. They also use the traditional Pagan names for holidays such as Yule, Sowan and Ostara.

"But what if people don't know how to pronounce the name Samhain?" asks Hayden, who is pronouncing it wrong.

"It's 'sow-an'," corrects Melissa, "like if you had a pig named Anne. And you're right; that one may deserve a pronunciation guide."

"Or a simplified spelling," Hayden persists.

The group debates the details of their calendar into the wee hours before reaching a consensus. [See Appendix A.]

Over the course of the next several weeks, Hayden works with Dennis and Diana to establish financial targets, and to set up websites and online payment accounts. It takes weeks of almost daily meetings, working late into the night while Melissa and Nicholas phone supporters and ask for donations of handcrafted goods to sell.

The next weekend is Thanksgiving, and the group elects to take the weekend off from their regular meetings.

By this time, several severe storms have blown by, leaving lakes in the lawns.

For Thanksgiving Day, Hayden travels with his lady-wife to her parents' house for a slightly awkward but ultimately enjoyable get-together with his new in-laws and their extended family. There is a magnificent old oak tree in their front yard. Hayden finds himself patting the tree for reassurance, each time he enters or leaves the house.

The weekend after Thanksgiving Day, the group meets again and resumes their work.

They are determined. They do what they must do. They get organized. They pursue the project with zeal, forgetting other commitments, spending their every waking hour working at it until it sometimes seems they are about ready to hate it, but no, it is still precious...

At last, their calendar is produced. Each month features a large print of an original painting, representing an aspect of a Pagan deity. It's a collaboration by an artists' collective, and each interpretation is different. There are several representations of Gaia, the Earth Mother, including her embrace with Sky Father. A couple of the paintings represent the freedom and abandon of wild nature, as personified by Pan and Kokopelli. Of the rest of the paintings, some of the deities are very Roman, a few are strongly Scandinavian; the image of Ostara is a bohemian hippie flower child; and one picture looks suspiciously like it's just a couple of fairies. ("Fairies aren't deities at all," grumbles Hayden, for which Melissa punches him in the arm.) The final painting in the collection touches on the intersection of science and modern Paganism: including a detailed representation of planetary orbits which on closer inspection might be electron fields, with some sort of mythical faces superimposed on the background.

They rent space and promote fundraising events: concerts, with volunteer bands; and dinners, cooked with donated food by volunteer kitchen staff.

At each of these events, Sage and Phoenix get up for some speechifying, reminding everyone who the group is, what they stand for and what they are trying to do.

One such fundraising event is their big Yule feast.

Chapter IX: Yule

The storms intensify as winter cracks down on those other seasons' frivolity. The first light dusting of snow falls in the week before Yule, but it has mostly melted away into thick slush before the time of the Winter Solstice Holiday. Rain pummels them on the drive out to their event.

The local Pagans have rented out a meeting space with a kitchen, just for the evening. Volunteers prepare heaping plates of pasta, scrumptious salads and delicious desserts. Community members contribute a minimum donation to attend, and a few drop sizable checks into the basket.

"Fire plays best around the edges," observes Nicholas.

"Yeah, especially when it's still just getting started," agrees Hayden. He and Nicholas are thinking of fire as an allegory for the fervor which they hope will sweep through the Pagan community and eventually ignite within the broader society. But the inspiration for their remarks is much more tangible in the present.

"We gotta plan this thing better next year," growls Dennis, as he fills the fireplace with wet wood, leaning the logs against the inner walls in hopes that they will dry out from being near the delicate flames that flicker around the edges of the damp fire as it hisses and smolders.

At last, with much blowing and fanning and cursing and

kindling, Dennis rouses a temporarily passable fire. He nods to Sage, who stands before the group and gets everyone's attention with a ritual bell.

"My fellows," she begins, "we meet this night to celebrate Yule as a community, as our families have celebrated Yule, by one name or another, throughout the millennia.

"Tonight we celebrate the Winter Solstice, the longest night of the year. Yule is an ancient tradition, and a time of hope. During the darkness we look forward to the return of the light. During the cold of winter, we rejoice in our families; and we rejoice in our community, which is our broader family.

"The entire Winter Solstice holiday season is deeply steeped in cultural associations of family and tradition. The Yule log is a symbol of continuity. The year lives and dies, but our community lives on. This log is a piece of the tree which we danced around last year. There in the corner is this year's tree. Next year we will begin our Yule festivities by burning the last log of this year's Yule tree, and perhaps we will recall this year's dancing and festivities. This is the tradition of the Yule log."[5]

Then Sage burns her Yule log from the previous year. Everyone sings a song, except for Hayden, who still can't understand why everyone else seems to know all these songs.

After this, Sage sits down, and there is a palpable excitement of tension in the room as the gathered audience awaits the speaker who they know will be next. What they

---

5　Some say that a proper Yule log should be a beech tree's slow-burning root, with a portion of the previous year's Yule log saved as kindling for this year's fire. However, I figure that it's best not to be pedantic about this sort of distinction, especially if you happen to live in a place where beech tree roots are not in plentiful supply.

don't know, and what's got them intrigued, is the open question of what it is that he will say tonight.

Once more, Phoenix gets up before the gathered group. This night his tongue flows even more freely than usual as he draws inspiration from a belly warm with mead.

"We are not unlike the first story-tellers," he begins. "Our ancient forebears sat around their prehistoric campfires and wove stories long since lost, about gods and heroes and monsters all long since forgotten. We can imagine that these long-forgotten deities live on, in some sense, because deities reflect natural forces and human concerns, and many of these concerns remain an indelible aspect of the human condition, even throughout dispersal over geography and time, and changes in culture and changes in technology and even changes in the climate, through the Ice Ages and now global warming; even though everything around us may be different in some ways, we are still people, and we must share an essence of humanness with even our most distant ancestors, just as we share an essence of humanness with even our bitterest enemies even today: for despite our other differences, we share the fundamental experience of human awareness, its sensations, memory, and emotions, love, loss, anger, loneliness, desire, fear, happiness, arousal, complex family relationships and cultural traditions based on stories and information passed along from one generation to the next. Maybe we all feel some sort of demons whispering in our ears sometimes, too: shame, guilt, and regret, unwanted thoughts, evil notions, even compulsive obsessions. And perhaps we all feel the opposite sometimes too: moments of profound holiness, resplendent with wonder and awe, when all is revealed and the infinite greatness of the Universe is laid out before you in a laughing-while-you-cry-because-its-so-beautiful connectedness, and all is revealed, and everything is connected, and you know beyond a shadow of a doubt that what you believe is right and good and true. This too is a part of the human condition. I think that certainly, most people have many of these types of experiences, at some time in their lives. Afterward, some people go on to become prophets, but most of us just try to get on with our lives as best we can.

"And throughout time, since long before what we have considered to be recorded history, people have had ceremonies and observances to honor the cycles and forces that influenced their lives: the seasons, the Solar and Lunar calendars, the forces of nature, and other energies and elements that remain inexplicable or beyond our control: fortune, prosperity, the availability of game animals, the success of crops, ventures, relationships; all that we desire and all that we fear, rolled up into a little bundle and trotted out for special occasions. But this little bundle of vague hopes and fears and misapplied incorrect assumptions regarding causality has a power of its own; and when the sum of these things is appropriated by a well-organized force and used with intent, it can become the justification for totalitarian control over the life of the individual.

"And this has been done repeatedly," Phoenix continues, the passion building in his voice. "Cultures throughout history and around the world have done just that: leveraged a religious doctrine combined with centralized power to exert totalitarian control over the life of the individual.

"This is the history of Abramism in all its forms. The followers of the god of Abraham believe that their beliefs give them the right to tell everyone else what to do, what to believe, how to behave. They think they can dictate to the rest of us what we are allowed to think. Their pogroms and purges and jihads and crusades have circled the globe over and again, terrorizing and torturing innocents in the name of their religion. They have done everything in their power to expunge Goddess worship and eliminate Paganism from the face of the Earth.

"But there were some cultural traditions," he continues, "that were simply too important to the local people, and could not be stopped so easily. For example, the people of the northern lands had celebrated Yule since time immemorial. The Solstice tradition can be traced back to the placement of the monoliths at Stonehenge."

"...and to every astronomically-aware civilization throughout global history," interjects Sage.

"The Winter Solstice is a time of rejuvenation," Phoenix goes on, "a turning of the solar tide, when the days begin to get longer, even though the bitter depth of winter is still upon you; so the Solstice is a time of hope, when you know you can look forward to a lifting of the darkness.

"Also, winter storms encourage feasting behavior and foster social cohesion. The season of inclement weather provides time indoors for making up songs and stories; so tradition sprouts out of tradition, and the winter holiday becomes an important life-marker for the entire society. The Church could not hope to ban such a deeply ingrained behavior, so they absorbed the Pagan celebration of Yule, the Winter Solstice. They renamed the holiday Christmas, and established a convention that the holiday was a holy day in their own calendar for different reasons. The holy writ is not specific on this point but it seemed like a judicious and political claim for the Church to make.

"And it worked! As long as people could keep their holiday, even by a different name, they were willing to abandon their Pagan faith and its connection to the natural world, in favor of a stronger god who made vague promises and threats about life after death. Eventually, dissenters were put to the sword, or the torch, or the rack, or the mill-stone; but for the transition, they were tolerated with good humor, like a poorly behaving child.

"The strategy succeeded brilliantly," Phoenix says bitterly. "All the most important holidays were co-opted by these well-funded, well-educated priests.

"Yule became Christmas. Immolc became Candlemas. Ostara became Easter. Beltane became Whitsuntide. Litha became the Feast of St. John the Baptist. Lunasa became Lammas. And Sowan became All Saint's Day.

"Major goddess deities were absorbed into the Catholic pantheon, with Brigid turned into a saint, and Eostar giving her name to an Abramist holiday.

"What was left that the Druids could offer the people anymore? In the free market of religions, the Druids filed for bankruptcy, allowing the Abramists to buy a monopoly position for pennies on the dollar.

"Christmas was possibly the Church's best-ever investment. With its existing theme of family closeness and cultural overlay of gift-giving, it has in modern times become a paragon of consumerism, and a significant driver of the global economy.

"And the Pagan culture was so completely subsumed that modern Pagans, seeking a way to spiritually connect with the multitude of divinities, the elements and the forces of Nature, were in some ways required to reconstruct the ancient rites from sources dating back a thousand years; and in many respects, we still make it up as we go along. That is how completely the Pagan culture was exterminated by the

Abramist culture war.

"But it's undying!" Phoenix suddenly cries out with passion. "The Pagans will rise again!"

A murmur of assent ripples through the audience.

Someone hands Hayden a large cow's horn filled with mead.

And the group communes around the Winter Solstice festival fire late into the night, as Pagans have done for millennia.

Chapter X: The Symposium

After Yule, they take the week off to relax and celebrate the dawn of the New Year.

Then they enter the month of Janus, and it's back to work. Now they must promote their artwork, baby accessories, kitchen accessories, and fantasy/fetish gear as everyday items, not just holiday gift ideas.

And they are somewhat successful. Not perhaps as successful as they might have hoped; but successful enough to be able to pay for a print run of postcard mailers with the proceeds.

"Not the nation-wide, pentagram-shaped recipient zip code concept that we were talking about before," Hayden explains. "That was perhaps a bit... fanciful."

"No, I understood you," says Diana.

"It's to notify the local mailing list about the upcoming parade," elaborates Dennis in uncharacteristic verbosity. Normally he sits silent through most meetings.

The meeting has been going for a while, and the mead horn has made many circuits around the room. Today's meeting has a less formal, more relaxed atmosphere, and the friends are all enjoying each other's company. Hayden and Marc share a nip of rum from a flask. While it's certain they all remember some of the tension that permeated their last meeting, nobody makes reference to it. Instead they focus on meta-questions: questions about questions, answers about answers, ideas about ideas. They are trying to solve the riddle of what a religion should be, and what spirituality should mean, so that they might determine how best to offer an ideal solution to the people of the world.

"What are people looking for in a religion?" asks Phoenix. "What do they get out of it? Why do they join, and why do they return to it?"

"To enjoy a sense of community," says Melissa.

"To connect with other people who share their core values," suggests Hayden.

"To seek solace in times of grieving," offers Sage.

"To look for hope when life seems to hold none," agrees Dennis.

"To participate in something larger than oneself," says Marc. "We seek a movement, a tradition, a unified people."

"To engage in spiritually transcendent moments," says Diana. "We wish to connect with our concept of 'the beautiful' and 'the profound' as we seek 'spirituality.'"

"To have an opportunity to reflect on life," says Dylan, "and to be grateful for life's blessings. To praise all that is beautiful in the world."

"To receive guidance in a confusing and sometimes malevolent world," says Nicholas.

"To have an excuse to sing in public," says Sage playfully.

"I wish we had better songs," remarks Marc.

"We need better songs," agrees Hayden. "That would be a great place to start."

"How could we ever agree on music?" objects Phoenix. "The members of this group would never all go to the same concerts."

"There's always hand drumming at the festivals," Nicholas

offers.

"That's true, but we're looking for songs that people can actually sing together."

"Well, *Circle Round* has a lot of songs..." offers Diana.

"Yeah, and those songs are great for singing with kids," says Hayden derisively.

"Hey, and a lot of grown-ups like them too," says Melissa, a note of warning in her voice tone.

"All right, granted," says Hayden, quickly backing down; "but I'm just saying that for me, personally, I'd like something with a little more soul."

"Wait, what?" asks Phoenix, laughing. "Are you saying that you want Pagan music to sound like Gospel music?"

Nicholas leaps to his defense. "Only in the sense that they're both participating in a larger musical-cultural gestalt," he says.

"But seriously," Hayden dreams out loud, "we could totally have like a blues band or something, leading the congregation in song to raise energy during our Pagan ritual services. We'll figure something out."

The rest of the group ignores this tangent.

"I think the important point to note here," Sage opines, "is that the various subgroups within a larger movement do not all need to agree on all the details, when they hold key fundamental principles in common. There are many ways to participate in spirituality and worship the Goddess."

"And that's just it," counters Phoenix. "Some groups might prefer not to focus on The Goddess at all, even if they pair her with her consort, The God."

"I like talking about the Goddess," says Diana. "It's nice imagery."

"Yes, it is," Phoenix agrees diplomatically; "and at the

same time, some people may take it too literally, and start weaving Goddess worship into some sort of dogmatic faith-based malarkey."

"Of course some of them will," says Sage sharply. "Do you really want to stop them?"

"OK, fine, you're right," Phoenix backpedals, "they should be allowed to believe and practice whatever makes them happy. I'm just saying, that's not the path I want to follow with my own personal beliefs and practices. I want something that ties in directly with my life."

"And that's fine," Sage says more warmly. "Pagans don't all believe the same things. Pagans have never all believed the same things. The earliest gods were what you might call hyper-local spirits, and each tree, knoll, and grotto had its own. The people in the next valley over had their own, completely different local deities. As time passed, what with cultural intermingling from trade and warfare, one tribe's deities would become ascendant. But even where cultures share a common pantheon, different gods and goddesses all have their own cults, and their individual holy days."

"There are many different names for similar concepts," offers Nicholas. "Rather than the Goddess and the Horned God, some of us venerate Mother Earth, and worship the virility of Pan."

"Some people might not want to worship gods at all," suggests Hayden. "I think a lot of people would prefer to be honest and direct in their expression of worship. You know? They want to say plainly,

"I worship the Sun, which is a huge ball of hydrogen engaged in a massive fusion reaction that's been going on for billions of years. I worship the Moon, which is a planetary satellite made of rock, and reflects the Sun's light even during the dark night here on Earth. I worship the Earth, which is this unbelievably precious resource, with its oceans of liquid water and its atmosphere of breathable air. I worship the Earth, which grows the food that nourishes my body. I worship the Earth, and the incredible diversity of life that it supports.

"I give praise to the Sun, and the Moon, and the Earth, for being what they are. I don't need to anthropomorphize them, or ascribe them magical powers or mystical qualities. I do not believe that the Sun, or the Moon, or the Earth, can answer prayers, or grant wishes, or provide magical protection, or hear me when I talk to them. I most certainly do not believe that the Sun, or the Moon, or the Earth have the power to make conscious decisions. That is not in their nature. But it does not make them any less beautiful. On the contrary, I can appreciate the beauty of what they are, without the need to project my own petty, trivial concerns onto them.

"The Sun, and the Moon, and the Earth, and the solar system, and the constellations, are vastly bigger than I am, yet I am connected to them, because we are all part of a system, this massive system within a system, expanding ever outward, and ever inward, with a Mandelbrotelian sort of pattern repetition."

"Wait a minute, what?" says Dylan, who is always a good listener. "You're losing me."

"The Mandelbrot set?" interjects enthusiastic Nicholas. "Well, it's a mathematical equation, that when you feed different values to the variables and plot the results, the result looks like a shape, but when you try to examine the edges of the shape, you can descend into infinite complexity, because the edges have crazy crinkles, and those crazy crinkles all have edges with crazy crinkles; so it never has a final, definite edge, it just keeps going into infinity. It's like if you magnified a satellite image of a coastline, and then magnified it down to the seashore, and down to one specific section of beach, with its rocks and broken seashells and grains of sand, down to the edges of the waves as they break on the beach, down to the individual grains of sand, down to the way the sand's molecular structure stacks, down to the atoms, and the subatomic particles, and the energy field-waves that form the subatomic particles: this complexity goes all the way down past where we're able to analyze it anymore. It's a sort of allegorical model of the universe, with proximally repeated patterns based on fundamental laws."

"Why proximally?" prods Hayden for fun.

"Because the patterns are similar; but it's not an identical repetition. My theory is that you would see similar patterns when examining the universe at any scale: from the electron rings of an atom, to the planets of a solar system, to the suns in a galaxy, and maybe if you could look at it from far enough away, you might see that all the galaxies of the universe are all moving relative to each other in a pattern that follows similar rules."

"I have no idea what you're talking about," says Dennis quietly, "but it sounds beautiful."

"All right, though, here's the problem I have, and I don't see how to get beyond it," says Phoenix, who feels left out of the spotlight.

"OK, shoot, what's your problem?" asks Sage, who does not care so much.

"What would an ideal Pagan ritual look like?" he asks.

"Well," she responds promptly, "just like we were saying that not all Pagans believe the same thing, there's no reason to expect that all Pagans should practice their observances in the same way. You might have a lot of people who prefer to do all their observances privately. There has always been a lot of individualism in many Pagan rites: for example, leaving a personal offering at a grove or a shrine or outside one's door to please the wee folk. Asking for help from the ancestors or the animal spirits, the tribal totem or local gods. Offering up a prayer at mealtimes. What, you think the Abramists invented that? Puh-lease. People have been saying some kind of Grace since long before Abraham, I promise you. Meals are some of the most important rituals of our daily lives. In modern society, mealtimes are more important than ever, because they provide a space that is separate from the rest of the rush of a hectic life, when families can sit down together and exchange stories, plans and ideas.

"There are many opportunities for private prayer, personal rites, or quick ritual observances in a small group setting. A person can engage in rites, rituals and incantations when passing local features endowed with natural beauty; such as hills, mountains, valleys, sacred trees, auspicious rocks, lakes, rivers, streams, waterfalls, and oceans. In addition to prayer and group ritual, a person can celebrate her connection to the Goddess through songs, dancing, and the enjoyment of life!"

"OK," he grants, "so there are lots of ways that a lone Pagan, or a Pagan family, can intertwine their observances with their daily lives. But what about a group setting? I wouldn't want to insist that everyone should go; but I think a lot of people like to be able to go to some sort of weekly group ritual. In the Hindu countries, on the weekends the local villagers will all walk to local shrines and present offerings of incense and colorful pigments to the gods. The Buddhists go to the temple, listen to the monks chant, maybe spin the prayer wheels or walk thrice round the *stupa*; or maybe light a candle, or just sit quietly, depending. The Jews have weekly Sabbath meetings at the local synagogue; the Muslims have daily prayer at prescribed times and Friday prayer at the local mosque; the Christians have their various forms of church or Mass on Saturday or Sunday or whatever.

"The major religions all do something different and they certainly don't all agree with each other but the point is that they have regularly recurring rituals. Now, you could argue that in every one of these cases, these kinds of rituals are encouraged by the priestly class for financial motives; and you would have a valid point. But at the same time, in the modern era, many religious groups have toned down the guilt, and people flock to them. So it's not just that the priestly classes want people to participate in regular observances; many people seem to crave these sorts of regular observances. It gives stability, order, and meaning to their lives, provides a framework for their social interactions, and guides them as they face difficult decisions."

"Some Pagans get together for ritual on a weekly basis," observes Melissa.

"Yeah," says Nicholas, "but the ones who do that tend to focus on what might be described as occult practices: ritual magic, this sort of thing. And most of the Pagan rituals that I have attended largely draw on this same tradition. What's ironic is that the whole thing with casting the circle and calling the quarters, it's not actually a tradition that traces its continuity back to the ancient Pagan rites.

"In fact," Nicholas continues, "it's actually based on the writings of Gerald Gardner, who many people describe as being the founder of modern Paganism, or at least the popular Wiccan branch.

"You see, Gardner was a Freemason; so the Pagan circle-casting ritual is essentially the same as the old Masonic Lesser

Banishing Ritual. He did make some changes, like the spirit names of the four corners of the compass, which had previously been the Archangels of the Abramist tradition. All this derives from the Hermetic Kabbalah, even though only a few people really get into all that."

"Yeah, you get into the Kabbalah, and it begins to smell like dogma again," objects Marc.

"I agree," says Phoenix firmly. "The question is, how attached are people to the circle ritual? And if we were to consider discarding it, what ritual would we replace it with, that would serve the same function of delineating sacred spacetime?"

"It could evolve over time," Melissa speculates. "It could change depending on the event. It might be a personal preference."

"People like to feel that they're participating in the ritual," interjects Sage. "It's why Vatican II decreed that the Catholic Mass didn't have to be said in Latin anymore. It's why ceremonies involve call and response chants, like 'Hail and welcome!' or 'So mote it be!' or even, 'May the Force be with you,' 'And also with you.'"

"And again," interrupts Marc, "this comes back to the music. Music simultaneously delineates sacred spacetime, and provides a participatory ritual format."

Ignoring the interruption, Sage goes on. "Well, you could argue that our usual ritual has continuity with a tradition of a sort. And perhaps more importantly, you could argue that the Masons and the Hermeticists have been doing it for all this time because it works on some level."

"Or," says Phoenix loudly, leaping to his feet and pacing across the front of the room, "you could say, leave the occult stuff to the occultists, and maybe start a new branch of

Paganism that's more accessible to a broader segment of society. Create new traditions based on our own self-image."

"What is this now, Pagan church?" demands Marc.

"A Pagan church is called a temple, or a shrine. But yeah, sure. Why not?"

"Well," Marc answers, "there was that conversation we had earlier about taking over, only to become that which we most despise about our enemies."

"What, murderous dogmatists?" exclaims Phoenix. "May Thor strike me down!"

"And then there's the most fundamental aspect of continuity in Pagan traditions," says Diana softly.

"What's that?" Phoenix asks.

"The nature tie-in."

"Now, *that* is an excellent point!" shouts Phoenix, excitedly. "Paganism around the world has largely evolved from a personal relationship with the land. People throughout the ages have been intimately familiar with the sacred places in the areas where they lived. They went to those places: to the majestic trees and the gentle springs, to waterfalls and hillocks, glades and groves. They went to these natural places, and they communed with nature, and perhaps offered up a prayer of some kind to the old gods: the spirits of the place. I think prayer of this kind can be very effective, as a way to focus the intent of the individual on the purpose of achieving a specific goal or state of mind, or of expressing well-wishes for a loved one."

"Right, fine," says Marc, in a hurry to get back to the point, "but the merits of prayer aside... It sounds to me like you are objecting to the circle ritual because you think the proper practice of Paganism involves the appreciation of the beauty of natural features. The problem is, in order to effectively compete with the Abramist religions, any hypothetical new branch of Paganism would by necessity have to move indoors, to some sort of temple: a space functionally similar to a chapel or cathedral."

"Yeah, that's right," agrees Dennis, breaking his characteristic silence. "If we're going to grow the community, our rituals can't always just be in somebody's back yard, or at the park. That's fine for small groups; but if you want the group to grow past a certain size, you need a formal space that can accommodate them all."

"But do we really want to grow that big?" asks Marc.

"Yes," pronounces Phoenix. "We do."

"I'm not sure I do," Marc maintains.

"Come on, man," says Phoenix impatiently. "Play to win, or don't bother playing."

"That's not what I'm looking for in my spiritual life," Marc explains. "For me it's not about winning a competition. It's about the pursuit of a higher self. I don't need to convince anyone of anything. I don't care what they think. I'm not living my life to please them. It's none of their business. Fuck 'em."

"Tell us how you really feel," says Diana.

"All I was trying to say," Marc continues, "is that moving indoors should not be necessary; or at least, not into a room that looks like an Abramist church. If you expect people to show up when it's rainy or cold, you have to provide a comfortable place for them to meet; so natural features are only appropriate meeting places for festivals in the warmer months."

"You could build a big bonfire," suggests Dylan.

"You could, and in fact you should, at the outdoor festivals; that's part of the tradition," says Sage.

"Bonfires contribute to greenhouse gas emissions," objects Melissa.

"You can never please everybody," sighs Hayden. His pregnant wife gives him an elbow in the ribs.

"Listen," says Phoenix in a vision-trance, "the point is, this is an opportunity to draw upon a different model. In many of the Eastern religions, a shrine might be located in a special or auspicious place, or combined with a natural feature. Like, a stupa might be at the top of a really tall hill, and in order to get to it you have to climb this huge staircase, so that you really have to physically exert yourself just to reach this place, and going through this exertion means that you have altered your state of mind by the time you get there, and ensures that you value the experience more, since you had to work to get it."

"That's great for a thousand-year-old temple in south Asia," Marc pouts, "but in modern-day America, that type of arrangement simply wouldn't meet ADA requirements."

"Right you are," Phoenix admits. "But it's just something to think about. A perspective, a different framework."

"Yeah," Hayden interjects. "When I was in Nepal, I once saw a Hindu shrine that was admittedly quite small, but it was in a lake, on this little tiny island that was really barely more than a rock, and you had to cross a small footbridge to get there."

"Oh, that's an excellent example," says Sage gleefully. "Again, this type of footbridge you describe physically separates the sacred space from the normal flow of daily life: you must reach it and leave it again by a special path. You can't just wander there accidentally. You mentally prepare yourself to reach the special place, before you actually get to it."

"Yeah," Hayden goes on, remembering, "there was

another one that you could only get to in a rowboat."

"In a rowboat! That's an even more complete separation of mentality through physical separation."

"But again, not ADA compliant," Marc grumbles.

"It's an interesting conceptual approach, though," says Nicholas, contemplative. "For one thing, a shrine of that size does not facilitate large group gatherings. It's not designed to have some sort of patriarchal ritual, where one person lectures the group, and assumes the role of an instructor, or a sort of intermediary between the individual and the divine. A shrine that size provides a direct line between the visitor and the spirit who dwells in that place; no human intermediary is required."

"It's true. There was only room in the shrine for one person at a time," Hayden explains. "People were lined up to take turns."

"Oh, how wonderful," gushes Sage. "That's the epitome of the individual relationship with the divine. It's such a personal experience that other people aren't even in the room with you. It's just you, there, alone with whatever it is that you consider to be holy.

"And that's what's so great about paying one's observances at a natural feature," she continues. "Just go to a mountain, or a river, or the ocean, or a canyon, or whatever local scene of natural beauty inspires you. You don't need a shrine. You just need to be present, and you automatically have a direct line to the most powerful forces of nature."

"Objection," says Marc.

"This isn't a court of law, but OK," says Sage, and yields the floor.

"Well," says Marc, walking to the fore, "I think it's important to remember that not everybody necessarily wants to be alone with the divine. It can be kind of a scary experience.

People have been scarred for life, even driven mad by divine revelation. Becoming self-aware might really suck for some people. Some people just might not naturally have as strong a capability of initiating a connection on that level. These people might actually really prefer to have an intermediary, some sort of Druid or high priestess or similar leadership figure."

"Oh, I agree," says Phoenix, secretly amenable to paternalistic ways of thinking. "Not only that, but the individual level of communing with the divine does not provide the same level of community feeling that you get in a group setting."

"Well, it has a different objective, and it serves a different purpose," says Marc, returning to his seat.

"Absolutely," Phoenix goes on. "But I think what we're probably going to be looking at, if we want to grow a major religion, is going to have to be some sort of ritual that incorporates elements of the group teaching tradition, where one or more speakers makes a presentation or facilitates a discussion of some kind. This could be some sort of passion play, or a ritual sacrifice, a ritualized invocation of some kind, or just a sort of philosophical lecture. You don't want it to be too dry though. You want it to be relevant. You want to touch on the themes of people's very real, personal, daily lives. There are the major life events: marriages, births, deaths. There are the holidays: the eight Sabbats plus Lupercalia."

"Lupercalia?" asks Hayden, trying to remember where he's heard the name before.

"Sure," says Nicholas. "The Abramists call it Valentine's Day. The militant ultra-conservative Hindus in India have declared war on it. The holiday has always been about the relations between the sexes, but the notion of romantic love is a relatively recent overlay. In the old Roman days, it was a fertility ritual."

"Right," says Melissa, wistfully. "All the beautiful young men ran down the street, half-naked and oiled, flogging the women with leather thongs."

"I don't think that would fly, these days," says Hayden doubtfully, with perhaps a hint of possessiveness in his voice.

"No," agrees Diana ruefully. "Greeting cards are the best we're going to get."

"Come on, at least some flowers and chocolate," chuckles Sage.

"Whatever," cuts in Phoenix dismissively.

The dismissive tone makes Hayden recall that he's never seen Phoenix with a girlfriend. There may have been one or two brief hookups at the festivals, yes, but nothing that lasted. Whether it is cause or effect, Hayden is unsure, but he feels certain that Phoenix's dismissive attitude towards romance must hold a key to understanding his nature.

"Anyway," Phoenix continues, "the point is, once you have rituals other than holidays and major life events, you're getting into participatory spiritual exercises for their own sake, as an end unto themselves."

"Right," says Sage, taking charge, "and that gets back to what we were saying before. What is the purpose of participating in the rituals of a spiritual community? We seemed to agree that a single given ritual might have many different connotations or purposes for the various participants, depending on their state of mind and other life factors. Different people who show up on the same given day might be in a state of joy, or sorrow, or whatever. But despite their differences, they are seeking a unifying experience: something they can share with their fellow community members."

"The question is," says Phoenix, "what brings the

community together?"

"I submit to you," says Nicholas, "that there is a fairly well-established framework for this type of group experience. The ritual typically begins with some form of ceremonial invocation. Next the speaker delivers a soliloquy, pondering the topic of the week. Morality, charity, life's little mysteries, our triumphs and tragedies; the human condition in all its wonder and decay. This is followed by the main ritual sacrament. To close the event, the speaker offers another few words of community, and near the end might even add some public service announcements, upcoming community events, fundraisers and action committees, this sort of thing. A final blessing and then people are free to leave or mill about as they please."

"Really?" objects Marc. "You would make a Pagan get-together follow the same format as my Grandma's church?"

"It would make it easier to assimilate your Grandmother, and win her over from her existing church," Sage points out.

"And the sermon?" Marc queries, expecting to catch her unprepared.

"I think there are an infinite number of themes," she answers spryly. "Discussing the importance of goddess worship could be one theme. Possibly it could tie in with an example from historical multicultural mythology, calling to mind a relevant story about a goddess from Sumeria, or Africa. Possibly a new mythology could be invoked, since the participants do have a shared mythology of popular culture, for what that's worth. I think it's important to discuss issues of morality, and invoke righteousness, and discuss these things in such a way that makes people feel good about their decisions, or resolve to make better decisions."

"But obviously you'd have to address these issues with

enough tact that you don't alienate substantial segments of the community," muses Dylan. "After all, this is a group with some flexible ideas about morality."

"No, I don't think so, not really," Sage demurs.

"Seriously?" asks Hayden, thinking of the open marriages he has been made aware of since joining the Pagan community.

"Absolutely," Sage maintains firmly. "Because on a fundamental level, I think most of the members of the community believe in core values like respect, tolerance and honesty."

Sage notes the look on Hayden's face, and addresses his skepticism directly. "I assume your incredulity is directed at sexual morality?" she says. "Yeah, you know what, it's true: there are some swingers in our community, and they make an outsized impression. But it's not really that important. Real morality, basic morality, the 'be kind and honest and fair to your fellows,' type of morality, is if anything stronger in the Pagan community than in society at large.

"I'll tell you what is important," she goes on. "Our culture of tolerance attracts people that the broader society rejects; and that must always be one of our core strengths. I think most people eventually realize that, broadly speaking, the swinger lifestyle does not usually facilitate healthy long-term relationships. For those who want to experiment with it, and for those few who can make that lifestyle work for them, who are we to judge?

"Really," she concludes, "most of the people in the community are more or less pretty normal; and as the movement goes mainstream, the proportion of community members with fringe lifestyles will represent a smaller proportion of the group as a whole. Please don't get me wrong. I love those people and I want them to continue to be part of the group. I don't think we should start getting all judgmental. I think the freedom to make personal choices is imperative, just as I also think that honesty is imperative. Anyway. I also think the younger generations no longer consider questions of sexual taboo to be the overriding concern of their lives. They're a lot more interested in finding work, succeeding in life, making friends, being part of a community, maybe finding love and starting a family. That's what they want. And if we can give them that, then we have the ability to draw large numbers of people."

"I liked what you were saying before, though," says Phoenix to Nicholas, returning to the primary topic. "When you were talking about working within a familiar frame of reference. I think that might help. The more familiar the format, the more likely people are to accept it. Many of the people who ultimately rejected Christianity grew up in an environment that required them to go to Christian religious observances with some frequency."

"Yeah, that describes me," says Hayden, "but I always hated church. Absolutely couldn't stand it. So why would I want to re-create that experience and subject other people to it?"

"What did you hate about it?" asks Sage, prodding.

"It was boring," Hayden replies, "and it talked about a lot of stuff that just didn't seem plausible. I couldn't believe it."

"OK," says Sage, "now imagine you had a similar experience, in terms of meeting with members of a familiar community and sitting down to listen to someone talk about high-order concepts of ideals; only the difference is that instead of threatening you with the dogma of hellfire and eternal suffering, the person delivering the speech had talked about ideas that really resonated with you: human brotherhood, and our connection to nature and the greater universe."

"I'm having trouble picturing it," Hayden admits.

"And yet I'm sure it could be done," Sage maintains. "In fact, there is an offshoot of Gardnerian practice called Blue Star, that has a fixed liturgy. The rituals are carefully scripted, and performed word-for-word and motion-for-motion, every time."

"But is this really what we want?" Marc says, not mollified. "Do Pagans really want to have to start going to the Temple of the Thousand Gods and ritually chant the same damn verses every Sun Day, whether they feel like it or not? It seems like it would spoil a lot of perfectly good weekends, and make something less special out of what's now a really event-driven, loosely organized, nascent religion."

"Loosely organized?" asks Dylan with a smirk.

"All right, completely disorganized," says Marc, allowing himself a chuckle.

"That's more like it," Dylan agrees as several of the others join in the general laughter.

"We're getting better though," Diana proposes.

"Actually," says Melissa, "I think the importance of organization can't be overstated. I recently heard the saddest story. I have these friends who are a married couple. For months, they had been 'church shopping,' looking for a religious community to join. And they considered joining the Unitarians, because the Unitarians as individuals seemed to believe many of the same things that my friends personally believe. But in the end they rejected the Unitarians because the Unitarians are too disorganized, and my friends were looking for something that offered stability to their lives. So they joined the Catholic church instead. It's such a tragic missed opportunity for humanity, when something like this happens.

And things like this are happening all the time."

"That is a very important point," says Phoenix, holding up a finger. "People join religions for reasons other than dogma. They might accept the dogma, or part of the dogma, as a necessary condition of joining; but they really join because they want to be part of a community. In fact, I think a lot of people join churches, not for the sermons at all, but for the affiliated groups that you find in churches. The bigger the church, the more groups it has to offer, and the more specifically targeted those groups can be. They have youth groups and senior groups, women's groups and men's groups, expectant mother groups, bereavement support groups, groups involved in charity work, singles groups and married couple groups, even sports groups."

"So," Sage summarizes, "if we really want to offer a comparable experience to people who are considering joining a religious community, then we have to offer comparable lifestyle benefits. Our Pagan Temples must offer tangible benefits: consolation to the miserable; opportunity to the hopeful; and recreational fun times to everybody else. Not just fun times, but the opportunity to spend time with people who are similar to oneself: similar age, similar interests, similar views on many subjects. Joining a religious community provides the opportunity to make friends. And if we really want to compete with the Abramists for feet through the door, then we can't organize those kinds of groups as an afterthought. They have to be a core feature of our organization."

"It's a necessary point of parity," offers Hayden, who is flush with business terminology.

"Exactly," agrees Phoenix. "What he said."

"How about affordable daycare?" asks Diana.

"Yes!" responds Hayden with enthusiasm. "What better

way to keep working parents coming in your doors, day after day, than by offering them a solution to a pressing need? There is always a need for affordable day care. That's the kind of basic-needs program that gets people to become lifelong members of a spiritual community."

"How are we going to offer day care, and women's groups, and sports groups, when we don't even have a building to meet in?" asks Marc, still skeptical.

"It's a goal," explains Diana. "We're trying to get a detailed plan in place. Then we're going to raise the money to put our plan in action. It's called, 'strategy.'"

"I think it's called, 'endless talking and not getting anything done,'" Marc mutters.

Hayden laughs out loud. This Marc guy can be a pain in the ass, but he sure does keep the conversation lively!

"I was thinking about those friends of yours," says Phoenix to Melissa. "It's interesting that you said they joined the Catholic church."

"It's the world's biggest branch of Christianity," offers Nicholas.

"And I would argue that one reason for that popularity is because Catholicism is not truly monotheistic," Phoenix asserts. "In fact, modern Catholicism is a form of diluted Paganism without the social stigma. Nominally, only one deity is acknowledged; but in practice, Catholic doctrine includes an entire myth cycle based on a pantheon of lesser deities: archangels, devils, and saints."

"Yeah," interjects Hayden, "I was reading recently about the evolution of a new deity in Mexico, *La Santa Muerte*, Saint Death, the guardian of the worst sinners. Practitioners consider her to be a part of the Catholic pantheon of saints, although she has been officially repudiated by the Vatican."

"It's a great example," agrees Phoenix, "of how beliefs and practices continue to evolve in modern times, according to the situations and customs of the people, even within the nominal framework of Catholicism.

"Not only that," he continues, "but Goddess worship is a major feature of Catholicism. The Goddess has always been central to Catholic doctrine, in the form of the cult of Mary, the Mother. Catholicism is the most Pagan of the Abramist traditions."

"Outside of the Unitarians," quips Dylan.

"Will you stop with the Unitarian jokes already?" Marc retorts. "I'm not sure they even really count as Abramists anyway."

"I get to joke about Unitarians because I used to be one," says Dylan with dignity.

"The point I was trying to make," says Phoenix, "is simply that the Catholics might be good targets for conversion and assimilation."

"Really? You think so?" says Marc dubiously.

"Absolutely. Think about it. Here the Catholics are. Individual churchgoers are members of this religious group because of their own personal family tradition, and because of the structure it offers. But they look around, and they are increasingly disillusioned by the group's corrupt leadership and authoritarian structure. Catholicism has modernized its doctrine more than some of the other Abramists, but the leadership is still not changing fast enough to keep up with the attitudes of their own membership, and attendance in the developed world is falling as a direct result.

"The whole thing with the Pope just reeks of patriarchy; it's quite literally a holdover from a time when Christianity was a military empire. The Pope's relevance has passed. All the corrupt Cardinals at the Vatican are a bunch of slobbering, celibate old fools who claim to believe in this anti-sexual doctrine while they cover up for priests who molest children. They proclaim this great sympathy for the poor while they religiously enforce an anti-woman agenda that has the practical effect of forcing millions to live in desperate poverty. And to top it off, they continue to maintain the position that gay people should somehow choose not to exist, or something.

"No, the Catholic Church has failed to keep up with the times, and that's why a lot of Catholics would gladly jump ship if that had a viable alternative. And I think modern Paganism is the best alternative to offer them. Or at least, it would be, if we had a bit more structure to our organization."

"And without the corrupt leadership," reminds Marc.

"Of course. Our group must be transparently democratic and constitutional."

"Why exactly do you think Catholics would want to become Pagans?" interjects Hayden, who finds this a blatant contradiction.

"I'm glad you asked that," says Phoenix. His tone of voice prepares them for a monologue, and Hayden reaches for the mead horn. "It's because so many of their traditions are based on Pagan traditions. That means they would have an easier time making the switch. Plus their doctrine is so obviously based on ancient Pagan concepts. It's like I was saying earlier: Catholics are not truly monotheistic.

"Take the Trinity, for example. The mystery of a three-in-one godhead is reminiscent of many Pagan triple-divinity figures. There's the maiden-mother-crone Goddess mystery that we are all familiar with because it reflects the mysteries of our lives. But there's also the Moirae, the three Fates of the Greeks; the three Norns, who occupied a similar position in

Nordic mythology; and the Suleviae, the triple mother-goddess of the Celts, who was often accompanied by a triple male-god consort. The three-as-one trinity mystery of the Catholics was clearly adopted from Pagan tradition.

"Then, moving past the Trinity, you've got the Catholic holidays, which are all blatantly based on Pagan tradition."

"*Stolen* from the Pagans," pipes up Dylan.

"Stolen, indeed," agrees Phoenix. "Every one of their major holidays was originally a Pagan holiday. Christmas, Candlemas, Easter, Lammas, and All Hallow's Eve are nothing but different names for the ancient Pagan holidays of Yule, Immolc, Ostara, Lunasa and Sowan.

"And to top it all off, you've got the undercurrent of polytheism, where Catholics offer their prayers to a goddess named Mary and a whole pantheon of saints and archangels and what have you. The fact is, Catholics do not pray to a single god. They believe in a kind of a god-king who rules over a heaven of lesser gods.

"And why should they restrict themselves to a single god? Think about it. Saying 'Have no other gods before me' is not the same as saying 'I am the only god.' The First Commandment of Moses means only something like, 'Say my name first when you perform your sacrifices.' It is a directive of practice; not a stricture of belief.

"They pay lip service to monotheism," Phoenix concludes, "but in their hearts, the Catholics have already rejected the One God fallacy that is nominally the core of Abramist doctrine. They just need to admit it."

"All right, I'll add that to our To Do list then, shall I?" sneers Marc. "Convert all Catholics to Paganism. OK, duly noted."

"Well, we'll have to work on this too," says Dennis, who

has stopped taking notes, and is feeling done with the conversation. "This is a lot of good ideas for today."

Shortly after this conversation, Hayden is talking to his sister, and mentions that he's been spending a lot of time with the Pagans.

"The trouble with Paganism," comments Hayden's sister, "is that it's too structured for me."

"That's hilarious," he says. "Some of my friends would love to hear that. Our problem right now is trying to figure out how to provide more structure for those who want it. But *less* structure is always easy! You just... don't do the structured bit.

"Actually," he continues, "I think Paganism is whatever you want it to be. If you want to smile to yourself when you pass your favorite landmark, that's enough. You don't have to circle widdershins or remember the names of the spirits of the houses of the compass points. You can just feel a sense of connection to the natural world, and the larger universe around us; that's what it's all about."

"But all the things you have to remember?" his sister persists.

"You're thinking of Wicca," he tells her. "And you're right; Wicca does have some more sort of structured rituals. But that's just one interpretation. Pagan tradition is as ancient as humanity itself. There are many branches, and many ways to celebrate it."

"I think I'm already a Pagan," says Hayden's sister.

"Yeah," he agrees. "I think you are, too."

It takes several months, many long hours, and thousands of dollars in advertising, but the group begins to recoup its expenses and amass a general fund by selling outside the Pagan community to the general public as a whole. This brings in new money, and simultaneously raises awareness about their organization. They even begin to receive charitable donations here and there: mostly just $5 or $10 but these help a lot, and a few contributions of $20 and one for $100 really improve the group's total cash flow.

Finally they raise enough money to announce, promote, and hold their first big rally. The publicity is expensive; the permit is expensive; the mandatory port-a-potties are expensive; the required security detail is expensive; printing a bunch of signs for people to hold and putting together a bunch of costumes for people to wear is expensive; but they've now raised enough to cover all these costs.

In planning the event there is concern, because in some years the weeks around Immolc are among the coldest of the year. "Not a naturally auspicious time for a protest," observes Marc. Yet in a vote of community members close to the project, holding the event sooner wins with overwhelming support.

As the month of Janus wears on, the baby's arrival draws near. By now Melissa is very pregnant. Her body feels stretched, bloated, and contorted. She walks with an odd waddle, and never feels comfortable lying down. She is looking forward to the birth of the baby: the sooner, the better.

The women of the local Pagan community get together for a ceremony to bless Melissa and to prepare her for the experience of giving birth. Hayden drives her there beneath a waxing gibbous moon, visible in the afternoon daylight; but he does not stay for the ceremony. Instead he goes to another friend's house, where a "Men's Mysteries" event attempts to prepare him for impending fatherhood, chiefly through the consumption of alcoholic beverages. Eventually, someone else has to drive him home.

Chapter XI: Immolc

Hayden remembers that he has read, somewhere, that there are two types of father.   One kind of father will stay with his wife through her labor pains, holding her hand, mopping her brow, and ignoring the midwives should they ask him to leave. The other kind of father will ride out on the hunt the moment his wife goes into labor: stay away three days, spear a giant boar, and bring back its bloody carcass for a feast in his wife's honor.

As he kneels beside his wife and holds her hand, Hayden wishes for a spear, and a horse, and a forest where he could hunt a boar. A dead pig might not please his lady wife overmuch, but at least he would feel as if he were accomplishing something. Sitting here watching Melissa writhe and hearing her moan in pain through her contractions just makes him feel useless, overly aware of the utter futility of anything he might do. "You're doing great," he says, squeezing her hand, picturing the spear's sharpened point.

Later, Hayden writes in his journal:

> Immolc was a blessed day this year. Although the winter cold has not quite ended, its grip on the land is loosening. The sun broke through the clouds for the first time in weeks, the birds are singing, and last night, an auspicious child was born.

After the baby is born, the group conducts another ritual,

this one a celebration to welcome the new baby into the Pagan community and the world.

Other than that, the couple retires from community life for a few weeks. The community continues to organize without them. The new parents have their hands full, as new parents generally do; but they participate in meetings and rituals when they can, and some of their Pagan friends come over sometimes.

*   *   *

Because Melissa is in labor, the loving couple cannot attend any major events. But the rest of the community holds their first protest march on Immolc. They wish to use the occasion of the year's first Sabbat to welcome the return of Spring, and to remind their fellow Pagans that the trivial Groundhog's Day has deeper roots.

The sky is grey that Immolc day, but the mood is festive as a parade of partying Pagans marches down a central street in town, wearing wild costumes and carrying spiritual and personal slogan signs. The event's own organizers experience a sensation of unreality to see such a positive response from the community.

The local Pagan community shows up in force, and many of their friends, all dressed as fairies and clowns, trolls, cavemen, and flowers; stilt walkers, people in masks, jugglers; and of course, many simple children of the Earth Goddess, dressed in their daily casuals. They are all smiling, many dancing, some singing or playing drums, guitars, flutes, trumpets, saxophones, all manner of wild carousing up and down the line that stretches along for several city blocks.

"Love your Earth Mother," say their signs. "The Goddess

is Alive," say others, "Magic Happens." Some other signs are more political, asserting First Amendment rights and even claiming Paganism as the world's oldest religion.

The permit allows up to three thousand people. More than six hundred people participate (although afterward, the local police estimate the number at fewer than three hundred). There are some two hundred additional onlookers: curious passers-by who watch from the sidelines, and a few community members who show up to show their support without actually marching.

Signs, masks, costumes, stilt-walkers, and jubilant noise. The Pagans make a statement and get their message out. They are there to put on a demonstration: a show of force. The hundreds of participants move like a tidal wave. The event feels like a big success and everybody has a great time. They walk slowly along their assigned parade route, some of them dancing as they go; then they congregate in a local park for speeches and socializing.

Sage gives the headline speech at this event, and she chooses to focus on the history and significance of Immolc.

"The cross-quarter Sabbat at winter's end, later renamed as Candlemas and still later observed as Groundhog's Day, has deep roots as a Pagan fertility ritual. Immolc is the traditional beginning of springtime. The name 'Immolc' is derived from the term 'Ewe's Milk,' because this is the beginning of the lambing season. It is the feast of the goddess Brigid, and the holy day is often called by her name.

"In order to gain an initial foothold on a Pagan society," she continues, "the Church was required to contend with existing beliefs. Some gods and goddesses from the Pagan pantheon were absorbed into the roster of the Christian Saints. That's what happened to the goddess Brigid. Brigid was an

Irish goddess of motherhood, the hearth, fertility and creativity. After the Abramist invasion, she became Saint Bridgette, the patron saint of the home; and her feast day, Immolc, which is also known by her name, became the Christian holy day called 'Candlemas.' In modern society, Immolc is commemorated as 'Groundhog's Day,' but this triviality belies its true significance, for it is an ancient Pagan holiday of deep importance. We sanctify Immolc as one of the cross-quarters: for this day is the midway point between the Winter Solstice and the Vernal Equinox.

"It's common," she continues, "for the gods of the conquerors to reduce the vanquished civilization's gods in stature, just as the Pictish gods were miniaturized by the Gaels, and transitioned from primary deities to pixies and spooks."

"It's worth noting," Nicholas mentions aside to a person who happens to be standing there, "that the Irish Gaels called this cross-quarter day Oimell; still meaning 'ewe milk.'" The stranger politely says, "Oh, really?" and goes back to listening to Sage.

Not everyone is so attentive. The local media, although notified ahead of time, resoundingly declines to cover the event, except for a volunteer from the local community radio station, and one independent blogger.

But those people publish stories about the event. The event's participants share their own photos, and the published media accounts, with their friends; and those friends pass it on.

On the Internet, the story spreads outside the local community through blog mentions and social media shares. The event even gets a nickname: The Rise of the Pagans.

Chapter XII: Under Fire

Mostly the people who show interest in the story are other Pagans. Across the country, Pagans and members of alternative social circles begin sharing the story with each other. But it never gets picked up by the mainstream media, not even the "Odd News" on Reuters. No jokes are made about the event by John Stewart or Peter Segal.

There are some people far outside the community who do notice, though. As word of the Rise of the Pagans spreads, negative attention flares up. The entrenched Abramist extremists, the dominant paradigm, those very same people whom the Rise of the Pagans was meant to protest against; they notice that there has been some dissent, and they are determined to quell it by any means necessary.

Hayden happens to be scanning through radio channels as he runs errands in his car one day when he comes across an angry voice saying,

"These self-described Pagans are not a legitimate religious organization. They are an abomination! They openly worship everything that is evil in this world. They wear devil horns for sport. Their Satanic rituals involve wild sexual orgies. They openly engage in the abuse of illegal drugs. They are not law-abiding citizens and they are not deserving of protection under the law! They deserve to be punished in this world just as surely as they will burn in the hereafter! Their evil, immoral, and illegal activities are not protected under the First Amendment. This group must be abolished, banned, disbanded; and its leaders must be arrested, incarcerated, and put to death for their crimes!"

Hayden turns off the radio. He feels flushed, sick to his stomach, nauseous. His heart is pounding. He breaks out into a cold sweat. He calls his wife on his cell phone.

"These people want to kill us!" he says, trying to keep the panic out of his voice.

"You just now figured that out?" she says teasingly. "They've been burning Pagans at the stake for thousands of years."

"It was on the radio," he explains. "There was one of these right-wing talk show hosts, inciting violence."

"Well, that's a technical term. Incitement is against the law. Was it really incitement?"

"He said we should be put to death."

The Pagans figure out which radio station had broadcast the show, and who the hate-spewing talk show host had been; but they decide against writing a letter of protest directly to the station, with the logic that, as Nicholas puts it,

"It's a pointless security risk. They don't give a shit what we think, and we'd just be giving them our names and addresses."

In the wake of this outpouring of anti-Pagan venom, members of the Christian community write angry letters to the editor of the local newspapers, as well as letters to the Mayor and the City Council, complaining about the perversions that are allowed to walk in the streets.

In defense, Hayden crafts a press release and sends it to the local media. The press release is titled, "Local Spiritual Leaders Respond to Threats." In the press release, Hayden interviews Sage and Phoenix for their responses to the hate-speech of the right-wing talk radio host. They assert, briefly, that they are a peaceful, law-abiding group, and that their traditions, beliefs, and religious practices are indeed protected under the First Amendment.

The press release concludes:

> It is not merely incorrect: it is offensive and indeed threatening of the far-right extreme fringe to deny that we have First Amendment rights. The protections of the Constitution extend to all Americans: even those whom one may disagree with. First Amendment rights are certainly not the exclusive purvey of the Abramist Fundamentalists alone.

Local media, of course, does not care. The local papers print the angry letters to the editor from the Christian totalitarians, but decline to run the official response from the Pagan community. A couple of local Pagans make obscure posts on their own personal blogs, but that's as far as their side of the story gets.

Meanwhile, the radical fundamentalist Christians post their anger to certain dark website forums popular with the neo-Nazis, who take up the cause.

Within days of the radio broadcast, the websites used by the Pagans to raise funds come under repeated and sustained attack from hackers. The group's main website becomes periodically unusable as it suffers from Distributed Denial of Service attacks. As a result, the group's web host kicks them off the server and they're forced to start paying substantially more to host the website with another company. Moving the site and restoring from a backup takes a lot of time and results in lost content.

Then the hackers find a security vulnerability and gain root access to another of the group's websites: the popular one that sells baby clothes. Once the hackers get in, they deface the site by replacing the homepage content with obscenities and racist slurs, images of Nazi symbols, and text advocating violent fascist white-supremacist extremism. Then the hackers use the web server to send spam. Getting everything re-set is a pain in the ass and forces the group to spend countless hours cleaning up the mess.

But it doesn't end there. The nonprofit's business registration is filed in the name of Dennis and Diana, and lists their home address. Beginning with this information, someone manages to acquire other personally identifying information, including Dennis's date of birth and Social Security Number, from a black-market online database. Then, impersonating Dennis, the thieves take out a credit card in his name, and rack up thousands of dollars in charges. The first he hears of it is when collections agents start subjecting him to threatening phone calls. The collections people call persistently, throughout the day, every day, sometimes in the very early morning or late in the evening, even on the weekends. He is able to fight the charges and get the line of credit reversed, but in order to stop the collections calls, he has to actually stop owning a phone for a couple of months.

And while all of this is going on, Dennis and Diana's house is vandalized repeatedly. A rock is thrown through their window. Shit is smeared on their front door. Their mail box is even set on fire.

But the authorities, although they claim to be sympathetic, treat the events as isolated incidents. They take reports and file them away but do not pursue them. Dennis insists that all these incidents are connected: that he is the victim of politically motivated, religious hate crimes. The police flatly deny the possibility.

"It's just a coincidence," the officer tells Dennis after the latest incident. "The vandalism is just some local kids, and the identity theft and the hacking stuff is all probably the Russian Mafia."

"The Russian Mafia would have tried to use my website to sell fake Viagra. These hackers were neo-Nazis."

"Pranksters," says the cop, checking the time.

"But it just keeps happening," he insists. "There are so many incidents, one thing after another."

"I'd be paranoid too, if all that happened to me," agrees the officer, trying but failing to sound sympathetic. "But don't get carried away by conspiracy theories. Stuff like this happens to everybody these days. The fact that it's all happening to you at once, is just a coincidence."

"Really? My mailbox was set on fire. That's a Federal crime, isn't it? Somebody smeared shit all over my front door. I find it hard to believe that the local kids are doing this kind of thing to everybody on my street."

"If we find out anything, we'll let you know."

Furious over the inaction of the authorities, Hayden attempts to escalate the matter to the FBI on Dennis' behalf. He writes a letter explaining that hate crimes have been committed against members of a minority religious group; but the local field agent is not interested.

The group sends out more press releases, announcing that it has come under attack. As before, the press does not care. The announcements are ignored.

So they organize a second protest event, and schedule it for Ostara.

Chapter XIII: Ostara

By the time of the Vernal Equinox, winter's end is palpable. The air is warmer, even the rain is warmer; and the intervals between the rain showers have increased to the point where it is sometimes even possible to see blue sky.

Hayden and the other local Pagans find the best photos from the first event, and print them on postcards. They send out the postcards to their donors and their mailing lists. They send out e-mails to everyone who has signed up for their e-mail newsletter. They post to their organization's website and social media channels. They announce that there will be a second demonstration, bigger than the first. Motivated by the success of the original Rise of the Pagans, many more people turn out this time.

The parade is huge, and the celebrants are festive. The costumes are even more plentiful and more colorful than before; the signs more numerous. The parade route works around in a big circle, ending at the park where it began. Hayden and Melissa are able to attend this one, carrying their daughter in a sling. As the great mass of people gathers in the park at the end of the parade route, and before the crowd has time to disperse, Phoenix ascends a platform and begins one of his harangues.

"It's so good to see us all come together in celebration of our shared beliefs," he says. "I am Pagan! Hear me roar!"

And the crowd roars.

"Someday people will look back on Christianity in much the same way that we regard the religion of the ancient Egyptians: as a curiosity, a tale wondrous to hear, almost impossible to believe that people used to actually believe these things and take them seriously; and not just any people, but the most powerful people of their days, the leaders of the mightiest nations in the world.

"For since the days of the Pharaohs, no culture has been so driven by its obsession with the need to impose its concept of order upon the chaos of the world as the culture of the Abramists has been. The fanatic zeal of their early religion was welded to the regimented Roman society's scientific study of the pursuit of power and profit through total military domination. This combined force proved unstoppable: even when it was transformed, as it was by the first Muslims, when the Great Prophet Mohammed rode upon Medina and forcibly 'converted' Pagans by the sword."

"Converted them from living Pagans to dead Pagans," observes Nicholas.

"Indeed. Mohammed's adaptation of the Abramist philosophy was particularly suited to the Arab culture, but he understood perfectly the utility of combining religious zeal with politics, and he rode the wave of religious jihad to a position of power in his own day. Successive waves of Abramists swept northward across Europe, east into Asia, and eventually west across the great seas. They were always seeking new ways of imposing their tyrannical will upon what they perceived as the chaos of the world, meaning parts of the world that were not yet assimilated or under their control. To them, chaos and disorder were equivalent with unbelief, the great sin, the failure to follow the First Commandment, which notably does not deny belief in other gods, but only orders the Abramists to worship their own household god first.

"The chaos that the Abramists needed to subdue, was a whole world full of Pagans: people who did not bow to their one god. Looking around now, it is shocking how completely they succeeded. They were methodical, utilitarian, and brutally heartless. They have been relentless in their pursuit of any who dare to dissent... the pursuit, and extermination, of dissent itself.

"The northward trajectory of the spread of Christianity is a study in Machiavellian social warfare. Establish colonies. Grant small favors to important people to keep them on your side. Play your enemies against each other to keep them weak.

"In the early days, the spread of Christianity employed a two-pronged approach: Jesus at sword point, courtesy of the Romans; and of course the missionary tradition.

"The ultimate objective was nothing less than the total subversion of Paganism, and its eventual elimination. Incredibly, the Abramists succeeded in many places. Almost no relics remain from the rich heritage of the ancient Druidic traditions, or the older Pictish beliefs.

"When certain Pagan traditions were too powerful to be overwhelmed by force, they were absorbed. Christianity was a cultural amoeba. But the springtime fertility rites of the goddess Eostar would not be willingly abandoned by the Pagan citizens of the Holy Roman Empire. So the rites were simply repurposed: the theme of fertility was overlaid with a theme of rebirth, and a tradition was established that associated a Biblical story with Ostara to form the holiday we now know as Easter. The fertility symbols (the rabbit, the egg) have been retained; but for most people, their meaning has been trivialized, the symbolism forgotten by a world that has grown complacent.

Yet we Pagans know and remember that the Goddess is too strong to be eliminated by even the most totalitarian doctrine.

"As Christianity spread malignantly northward, it had to contend with the ingrained Pagan traditions. Initially, the Church tolerated converts who held dual allegiances with the local Pagan deities. The clergy were willing to make this deal with the devil, if it got people in the door, filled the pews and the tithing box; and more strategically, established a long-term foothold for the Church and its teachings.

"Then once it had a hold on society, the Church grew intolerant of dissent, and brought us the Dark Ages, while meanwhile the Abramists of the Turkish empire were making great advances in chemistry, mathematics and literature.

"With the contest won and the Pagans subdued, the Church cast about for groups of sinners against whom it might pit its ever-increasing might. Society looked inward, and began to persecute any whose behavior retained vestiges of Paganism. Ignorant plebians conflated herb-lore with witchcraft, and burned their wise-women at the stake.

"With much folk knowledge thus cruelly eliminated, the Church cast even wider for enemies. Eventually the armies of Europe were mustered to war against the Saracens.

"The Crusades foreshadowed the Military-Industrial Complex. The economic might of a state is aligned with its military interests. Not only is foreign conquest a source of revenue, but the endless preparation for battle is a reason to levy fees and conscriptions upon the local populace.

"Well, fast-forward to the modern day. The pretense of promoting democracy has been dropped from the rhetoric that is otherwise largely the same as it was during the days of the Red Menace. Everyone is now upfront about the fact that the cultural and military wars of the day are specifically about economics and religion. For economics, I give you the Tea Party vs. Occupy Wall Street. For religion, we have the anti-Western jihadis, the finger-chopping Taliban, and the African terrorist network whose very name, Boko Haram, translates roughly to 'Western education is sinful.'

"Ladies and gentlemen, the Abramists are still hunting witches. The same mentality executed Galileo, and Socrates before him, both for impiety, utterances against the gods, daring to voice possibilities that disagreed with the official dogma. And it's not confined to the Muslim Abramists. The Jews have their hard-liners as well, settlement-building Zionists and rabid religious hawks, bent on holy war. And of course the Christians have this deeply ingrained tendency to vilify science, education, and personal freedoms, presently embodied by the pushes against evolution and women's health care."

"Hear hear!" someone shouts.

"This is part of the war on Christianity!" shouts a heckler.

"No, this is a response to the Christian war on freedom," retorts Phoenix. "Christianity is the dominant paradigm. Christians constantly force their views on the public. It's ridiculous that they try to adopt this posturing like they're being persecuted, just because we don't all want to bow to their god."

"There is only one God! You worship Satan!"

"You don't even know what a god is. Why are you here shouting at me?"

"Because you're evil! Come to Jesus and save your soul!"

"You are lost, brother. Come to The Goddess and save your life!"

"The Goddess!" cries someone in the crowd. "The Goddess!" several other voices answer.

Without giving the heckler an opportunity to think of a

retort, Phoenix continues. Speaking directly to the heckler he says, "Your vision is one of religious totalitarianism. It's not compatible with the doctrine of freedom. You want to force my children to pray to your god in the public schools. You want to force me to worship your god at the beginning of any official government business. You want to display your religious symbols on public property, and you want the public to pay for them. And to top it all off, you want to use the government to take away the rights of women to make their own private medical choices. It doesn't stop with abortion: you would even force women into a subservient social role by denying them access to basic contraception."

"Contraception goes against the will of God!" shouts the heckler.

"The only thing it goes against is your totalitarian patriarchy. You will never accept the individual's right to self-determination. Whether the question is prayer or personal medical decisions, you want your Abramist Church to make people's decisions for them, and you want to use the government to force your religion on your neighbors. Reasonable people may be able to influence the courts, eventually, over the coming generations; and that's why I believe that eventually the individual's right to live in freedom from your religious persecution will be upheld. But you won't ever accept that you've lost the debate, both morally and ideologically. Instead you will never, fucking, let it go! You and people like you will rag on about it, as if it were still an issue. You will try to make an issue of it when nobody else cares. As far as you're concerned, nothing can ever really be settled, can it? Not unless you won; and you aren't going to win this; so you won't drop it for a thousand years. I can see it now. A thousand years of Christian terrorists, attacking police officers, bombing health clinics, murdering innocent civilians, all in the name of some inane point about personal medical choices! Your refusal to let this drop will inspire militant groups, white supremacists, all kinds of crazies, they will take up your rallying cry and declare war on peaceful people, wreaking the devastation of the Christian jihad against modern society for eons to come. Thank you, Jesus, for all the hate and suffering your followers perpetrate in your name! These militant groups are already increasing in number. Just check out the latest reports from the Southern Poverty Law Center, it's very disturbing. And you heard about these 'Sovereign Citizen' ass holes who think the law doesn't apply to them? Going around, shooting cops over traffic tickets and all that."

"But those aren't the same people..." the heckler objects.

"On the contrary," Phoenix shouts, "the crazy whacko extremist types are inspired by precisely this type of anti-choice rhetoric that's spouted by your foaming Abramist preachers. Do you remember on the news a while back, there was that right-wing group that was plotting an attack against the government? They were all about preparing for the End of Days, Book of Revelations style, and bringing about the Return of the Messiah by starting the War to End All Wars, which somehow had something to do with their plan to kill a police officer, and somehow this bizarre idea seemed perfectly reasonable to them.

"And as time passes, we're going to see more of it," continues Phoenix. "Evangelical Christians are the enemy of a free and open democratic society. They are happy to adopt the tactics of the extremist jihadis. Their Abramist belief systems are nearly identical. Christians and Jihadis both believe that any atrocity committed in the name of their God is automatically justified. It is the same Pagan-persecuting, witch-hunt mentality that has characterized Christianity from the Dark Ages and the Crusades through the Inquisition and the Salem Witch Trials. Need to sack a city? Blessed be the name of the Lord. Feel like burning your neighbors at the stake? Nice old ladies and herbalists? Hallowed be the deeds of the Lord!

"In the eyes of the Abramists, anything done in their God's name, any crime, any murder, no matter how foul, is justified by their twisted religious doctrine. The Christian terrorists who bomb abortion clinics and murder doctors are no different from the Islamic jihadis, who murdered thousands on 9-11, and who assassinate young girls just for going to school. It's the same Abramist doctrine of xenophobia and hatred."

Phoenix's voice soars as he cries out, "We are here to say that we've had enough of it! No more!"

"No more!" shouts Hayden. "No more!" shout others.

"Stamp out the scourge of Abramist religious totalitarianism!" Phoenix concludes. "Bring in a new era where differences are tolerated and even celebrated! Bring in a new world where people can live in peace! Give me freedom or give me death!"

And with that, the heckler shoots him dead.

Chapter XIV: Mourning

At first, no one seems to be certain that they are really seeing this happen. The shot is so loud that the sound doesn't seem related to their event. People think it must be construction noise from across the street. The heckler, now the murderer, calmly replaces his hand gun in his back pack and slips away through the crowd. Nobody stops him. They are all staring at Phoenix, who wears a look of stunned shock and pained surprise on his face as his body crumples in slow motion.

The police, when they arrive, do not seem to believe the onlookers who describe the assassin. They hardly take any notes or statements from witnesses, but instead interrogate members of the group that had sponsored the event. They detain Dennis and haul him down to the precinct office for a lengthy interrogation.

When they finally release Dennis, Hayden and Melissa go with Diana to pick him up from the police station. Melissa and Diana are still sobbing. Even the baby is crying. Hayden feels like he has hardened into stone. His brow is furrowed, his lips are turned into a snarling frown, and his mind is blank except for a red-hot point of rage just behind his right temple.

"What did they want?" he asks Dennis in a low voice, once the general emotion of the reunion has settled down a bit and the car is under way.

"They had this idea that the assassination had been staged as a publicity stunt," says Dennis, "and that I was somehow behind it. They would not accept any statements that contradicted their theory. To tell you the truth, I think those cops are all fans of that right-wing ass hole you heard on the radio. They just assumed that anything I said was a lie."

"Those fuckers!" Diana cries out with feeling.

"I'm pretty furious," Dennis agrees. "At first I thought I was supposed to be helping them catch the murderer, so I talked with them, and talked, and talked some more. I gave them a description of the guy who did it, and they didn't even take notes. Eventually I realized this wasn't getting anywhere, so I said if I'm a suspect then I need a lawyer. After that, they left me in the interrogation room by myself for another six hours; just forgot about me, apparently. Then eventually somebody came in and said I could go. By that point I was so glad to leave that I actually said 'Thank You.' Now I'm just so pissed off..."

The media coverage of the event focuses on the police theory that the murder was an inside job, staged for publicity. Members of the Pagan community are not asked for their side of the story; they are simply vilified in the press.

A few days later, the entire local Pagan community gathers at the house of Dennis and Diana for the ritual ceremony commemorating the life and death of Phoenix, who had been the group's charismatic focal figure for the past many years.

Outside, the birds twitter mournfully.

Sage leads the ritual. She casts the circle and calls the quarters; then allows them all to be seated. A hush falls across the crowd.

"The Universe is a whole unified entity," she begins. "It is a continuum of space, time, matter and energy fields. Life and consciousness are the products of chemical reactions based on states of energy and matter. When we die, our life force converts to a different state. The energy that fueled our life rejoins the larger energy field of the Universe. The matter that made up our bodies breaks down and rejoins the matter of the Mother Earth, to become part of the great cycle of life, and eventually to be incorporated into new life. We are all part of a great cosmic All, and upon our death, the boundaries and distinctions between ourselves and the Universe are eliminated. We become, more literally, a part of the whole.

"This is the transformation that our brother is undergoing. He has been taken from us, yet he is still with us, in a very real and scientific sense. We cannot talk to him in a way that he could hear us, for he no longer possesses an awareness. His life energy has dissipated into the infinitely larger energy field of the Universe. He has rejoined the Goddess. And because his life force has joined the Universal Force, we can know with certainty that his life energy is all round us. He is a part of the great universal energy field that literally penetrates our bodies with particles of solar radiation every day.

"Ritual sacrifice is among the most ancient and universal themes of human mythology. Before a hunt, the earliest ancients tried to propitiate the gods, the spirits of the ancestors, and the spirits of the animals themselves. More recently, the development of agriculture seemed to directly validate the idea of sacrifice: for it was by sacrificing the best of the crop, and burying it in the ground, that the next season's crop arose.

"The next season's crop arose from the sacrificed fruits of the last season's crop. It seemed directly observable that the gods approve of sacrifice, because sacrifice brings rewards, sometimes tenfold rewards. It's unsurprising that prehistoric people would have reached the conclusion that even greater sacrifices would bring greater rewards.

"The ancients thought of sacrifice in much the same way that we think of investment today. Sacrifice is a primitive form of investment. It is not without risk; but we give something up now, in hopes of getting back much more later. Sacrificing the best fruits to the Earth Mother could lead to a bountiful harvest if the rain was good.

"The observation of new life springing from dead matter inspired ideas of rebirth: temporal reincarnation, or even a spiritual afterlife.

"And thus there have been traditions of human sacrifice, sometimes accompanied by ritual cannibalism, around the world, for thousands of years. We don't talk about it often because we find it so disturbing, but the practice of human sacrifice was revived periodically throughout Classical Antiquity, until it was finally put down by the Pagan Romans just about two thousand years ago. In the Americas, the Aztecs were famous for their elaborate rituals. They carried on an extensive bloodbath of human sacrifice until only about 500 years ago, when their culture was utterly destroyed by the Spaniards.

"In some societies, once actual human sacrifice had been made taboo, some form of substitution was practiced: and instead of a person, they sacrificed livestock, a wicker man, or perhaps a loaf of bread baked into the shape of a human child.

"There are also many myths involving a god who is sacrificed, always for some higher purpose. After the god Osiris was murdered by his brother Seth, his wife Isis put him back together; and from his reassembled corpse she conceived Horus, who then became the king of the gods. In India, they have the myth of the god Manu, who was dismembered, and the parts of his body became the world and humankind. It's nearly identical to the Old Norse myth of Ymir, the frost giant, who was killed and dismembered so that the Earth could be made from his body parts. Norse mythology also tells how Odin crucified himself upon the World Tree to gain insight; and when he returned from death he was more wise and powerful than ever before. After he brought fire to mankind, the Titan Prometheus was bound to a rock, and his liver was sacrificially ripped out and eaten on a daily basis. The god Dionysus was torn to shreds by the Maenads during a particularly wild Bacchanal, but he returned again to party on." A few chuckles are heard from among the somber crowd.

"Adonis and Attis died and rose again," she continues. "The sacrificial death and subsequent resurrection of Mithras strongly influenced the Pauline doctrine, which eventually evolved into modern Christianity. And of course the dominant religion in our part of the world is based on a belief in a god-man who was sacrificed by his own father, and whose flesh and blood are regularly consumed by his followers in a ritual act of symbolic cannibalism known as the Eucharist.

"Now, as we stand here today, I tell you, Phoenix shall not have died in vain. His sacrifice, supreme though it was, allows him to number among the greatest and most revered figures out of legend. I don't personally believe in resurrection, reincarnation, or even an afterlife. I would prefer to have him with us today.

"But through his sacrifice on Ostara, he has been transformed into a symbol; and a symbol is a powerful thing. He shall live on in our memory. His passion shall live on in our struggle. He shall gain new life after death because we will fight on in his name!"

And she finishes off with an ancient verse:

"From the Mother he sprang,
To the Mother he returns.
In the name of the Mother,
Wassail!"

"So Mote it Be!" they all chant.

Chapter XV: Join 'Em

After these distressing events, everybody is a bit freaked out. Many of those who had been present that day feel the remorse of the survivor, and blame themselves for not stopping the murderer.

Wishing to be together with the community, our First Couple begins attending more Pagan meetings again, now bringing their baby along. They take turns being the one who has to leave the room when the baby gets too loud. At the meetings, a few people mutter darkly in corners about burning pentagrams on the lawns of their enemies; but the discussion never moves into action.

Meanwhile, Hayden writes a lot of letters: to the editor, to the police, and so on. He carefully crafts his statements, selects the recipients, tries to personalize the messages a bit, but hears nothing back.

All too soon, the Pagans hear from the police that the investigation into Phoenix's murder has been sidelined. Dennis gets the call, and Diana posts the news on Facebook. Melissa sees it in her feed and tells Hayden.

"The police say Phoenix's murder is a cold case. They're dropping the investigation."

Hayden spews forth a long string of withering curses. He takes a breath. "You've got to be kidding me," he summarizes. "Already? It's only been--"

"City Hall says they have more important things to do."

"Then I'm going to take over City Hall," says Hayden.

"You what?" asks Melissa. She fears that Hayden might be seriously contemplating a *Battle of Hillsboro* style all-out military assault on the administrative offices of local government.

"Yeah," says Hayden. "I'm going to run for office."

She breathes a quiet sigh of relief.

"I'm going to get elected as a City Councilor," he continues, "and then the police will have to do what I say."

"I'm not sure it works like that, honey..."

"I know. But still. I'm going to do this."

Hayden means it, and he decides to make a big formal announcement of his decision to run for office. He finds his voice speaking before an assembled group of local Pagan community members.

He stands up before the gathered group and feels his heart pounding. He chuckles nervously, shifting his feet; looks at the floor, looks up again. A low conversation has already sprung up on one side of the room.

"I feel like it should be Phoenix," he says, "and not me standing up here in front of you all right now. I remember listening to him as he stood right here and spoke to us, and I never, ever would have imagined things turning out like this.

"So, some of you may know, that Dennis and I have been in touch with the police. We've encouraged them to devote resources to this and treat it as a politically motivated assassination, or a hate crime, or something. But they don't seem willing to move past their original theory that the murder was some kind of fucked up publicity stunt. So anyway, the case landed on the desk of some overworked detective down in homicide. He's got nothing to go on, it's just another case in his file, and the DA is breathing down his neck on some other case, so this one is simply not a priority for him.

"But I was both saddened and disquieted when I heard from this detective that the case was officially being back-burnered for lack of evidence: filed under 'cold case' and left there. Well, that set me off."

"Yes it did," Melissa speaks up from the audience. "That set you off all right."

He gives a low laugh and goes on. "So I wrote a bunch of letters. I explained how much evidence had never been gathered, all the people who had never been interviewed. Had anyone in the audience been filming? What about security cameras on the buildings across the street from the park?

"It was so soon after the murder, I couldn't imagine that the case would be cold already. I felt like they were giving up too easily.

"Naturally, you can guess what kind of a response I received... none at all. Nothing.

"And that's why I've decided to run for office. Because Phoenix deserves better.

"In a country built on ideals of religious tolerance, why have the police failed to investigate the heinous public murder of a spiritual leader? Is it because he is a member of a minority religion? If religious concerns are influencing the workings of justice, then I believe new leadership is required. It's time to change the way things are done in this city!"

His candidacy electrifies the local Pagan community. But he doesn't spend a lot of time playing on sympathies, or posturing as some sort of conspiracy victim. He does not go around saying, "oh woe unto us, the poor oppressed religious minority..." - no, after that one speech to the Pagan community, he rarely brings it up again. Instead he tries to talk about his goals — things that he wants to see happen for the district.

He talks about the importance of the seat he is running for, and how it is involved in decisions that affect the people in his district. He details specific actions he will take to improve district residents' lives if he is elected.

It's difficult, but he goes out and talks to people. He attends City Council meetings. He goes to School Board meetings. He tries really hard to remember people's names, and to speak about their chief concerns. He has to remember to listen, to be responsive and still be assertive. It can be a fine balance, and he makes his share of *faux pas*. He tries to laugh them off and apologize, and most people are generally understanding. He does tend to berate himself afterwards; and moans at length to his patient, supportive, loving wife in the evenings after his meetings.

After all the paperwork has been filed and his candidacy is official, Hayden sends out a bunch of mailers to build awareness. But that isn't all. He goes out and knocks on doors. It takes weeks, and requires him to speak to many people who are very rude; but he shakes hands with someone from most of the households in his district.

In the election contest, his main opponent is an entrenched incumbent with a history of advocating prayer in public schools. So when they have a debate in a public forum, Hayden brings it up.

The debate has already gone on for a while, and seems to be winding down, when the moderator asks Hayden to summarize what differentiates him from his opponent.

"My opponent backed an initiative to mandate religious observance in public schools," he says in reply. "That is a form of totalitarianism. By way of contrast, I believe in freedom of religion. So I think that's a pretty important distinction."

"It's part of the War on Christianity!" shrieks the other. "The fascists won't let our children pray!"

"No," maintains Hayden calmly but firmly. "This is radical Christianity's war on freedom. Anyone can pray whenever they want, to whatever they choose. The difference is, you want to force *my* child to pray to *your* god. Talk about fascism: you want to dictate which belief system is taught in the public schools.

"You're the one waging war," Hayden continues. "It's the war of the totalitarian theocracy against the freedom of the people. It's the war to eliminate our First Amendment rights. You want to dictate what everyone else should believe."

"Hold thy tongue, Satan spawn!" spits the political candidate at the other podium. "I've heard all about you and your devil-worshipping friends. You should be locked up in jail."

"You want to imprison me for my beliefs?"

"You worship evil!"

Hayden looked at the moderator. "This is off topic, but I'd like to respond to this personal attack," he says.

"Please keep it brief," says the moderator.

"Well, my opponent's characterization is ludicrous, and it deserves a response; because now people will be wondering what it is that I believe."

"Go ahead," the moderator prompts again, looking at the clock.

"I'm a member of the Pagan community," he says in an uncertain voice, then hurries ahead before his opponent can interrupt. "We celebrate the changing of the seasons. The holidays you call Easter, Halloween and Christmas are all Pagan holidays. So it's hardly... what my opponent claims.

"But my own personal spiritual beliefs and practices are

not the issue here. The question is simply, whether I should be allowed to determine them for myself. My opponent supports dictating dogma. He thinks he can tell other people what they are allowed to believe. This election is about freedom for all. It's so basic to our culture, but this very freedom is under attack from totalitarian religious extremists: people like my opponent here, who want to force their views on everyone.

"I had a good friend who was murdered in public," Hayden continues, his voice ringing louder and the audience growing quieter. "He was assassinated for voicing his opinions. He was gunned down in broad daylight in front of dozens of witnesses for exercising his right to free speech. Yet the police have sidelined the investigation. They say they can't find the murderer. I say they don't *want* to find the murderer. They don't want to find the killer because," he pauses, looks at his opponent, looks at the moderator, looks at the audience, and speaks the words loudly, slowly, and clearly, "they believe that my friend deserved to die." He pauses again to let the assertion sink in, then goes on. "The police refuse to solve the murder because they approve of the crime. And through their refusal, the police are complicit in the murder."

The moderator cuts in. Turning to the incumbent, he says, "You have thirty seconds to respond."

"It won't take me thirty seconds," says the incumbent, filled with self-assurance. "The police are correct. The righteous do not tolerate Satan worshipers. *Thou shalt not suffer a witch to live!* The death in question was not a murder; it was a necessary killing to purge evil from our society."

Nobody says anything for a moment. The entire chamber is quiet.

"My opponent is on record defending the murder of anyone who disagrees with him," says Hayden into the microphone. "He is in favor of shooting people for their beliefs. I think that's a pretty clear distinction between us."

The people of the district agree. When the votes are tallied, Hayden has unseated the incumbent by a landslide.

Hayden does not make any sudden moves. He bides his time, and grows accustomed to his new position. Then one day he sits down at his desk and types up a letter that has been brewing inside him for a long time.

Hayden has written many letters before: to local media, and even to the FBI. But now he is a City Councilor, and his missives carry an added weight. He frames a very carefully worded official memo, thereby making the matter a point of official city business. He asks the local FBI field office to explain why the police closed a murder case without examining all available evidence.

Agent Sandstone is at his desk at the local FBI field office, working on something else, when someone brings him a letter from a City Councilor. This in itself is odd; most people just send e-mail these days. Agent Sandstone likes e-mail. It is easy to ignore.

Agent Sandstone scans the memo briefly, and tosses it aside. "Goddamn conspiracy theorists," he says to himself. There are murders every day. The police have limited resources, and they close cases for a myriad of reasons.

But as he is driving home that day, Agent Sandstone passes what appears to be the face of a goddess, outlined with flower petals on the side of a building. He is momentarily struck by the beauty of the face, before he recalls himself and remembers that such a public display of religious art on private property probably constitutes vandalism. Or is it vandalism, if it's made of flower petals? They will wash off the next time it rains. Anyway, whoever put the petals there was trespassing.

The next morning, stuck in traffic, annoyed at the radio, Agent Sandstone follows a flock of birds with his eyes, and is suddenly struck immobile by the sight of a face in the clouds. He is certain the cloud formation looks exactly like the face of the goddess from the building yesterday. She is so beautiful, he forgets to drive. Another car honks. He lurches forward, and suddenly he begins to wonder, purely from a practical standpoint, "How would I be able to tell if the police had helped cover up a murder?"

Later that day, when he has a moment, Agent Sandstone begins asking a few innocuous questions about the case. The answers are somewhat unexpected; and they lead to more questions. These answers eventually lead to subpoenas, and the subpoenas lead to arrest warrants and a criminal complaint.

Eventually the FBI raids City Hall and hauls the Police Commissioner in front of a Federal Prosecutor on charges of Obstruction of Justice, and Conspiracy for his alleged links to the neo-Nazi fascists who had been persecuting the Pagans.

The complaint alleges that the police chief and several of his officers had engaged in a conspiracy to protect the identity of a murderer.

Eventually the FBI is also able to locate Phoenix's assassin, based on information retrieved from the Police Chief's laptop. After an armed standoff with a SWAT team, the assassin fails to provoke the shootout he had hoped for. Eventually the man commits suicide rather than stand trial for his crimes. He leaves behind a note explaining that his only regret is that he had not killed more people in the name of Jesus.

Of course, all this makes quite a stir in the press. The public assassination of an activist who nobody has heard of does not matter to the media; but the arrest of a police commissioner on conspiracy charges is big news. There is an even greater stir in the press when it is revealed at trial that the police officers are all active members of an underground right-wing extremist organization, and that they had actually acted on instructions from the organization's pseudonymous leader to shield the perpetrator, even though they were aware of the perpetrator's identity.

Meanwhile, all this press coverage helps the Pagan movement as a whole to grow in popularity. Many people begin to get interested. New covens and shrines spring up all over the country.

The local organization gets a windfall of donations. They use the money to buy a vacant church and convert it to a Pagan temple. First they smudge the area and conduct ceremonies to sanctify this hallowed ground in the name of the Earth Mother. Then they have a big party to celebrate their new sacred space.

Now that they have a temple of their very own, the local group no longer has to rent out a grange hall somewhere out of town whenever they want to have a ritual, get-together, or Sabbat feast. They don't have to invade Dennis and Diana's house, either. Now they have a place of their own, where they can host rituals and festivities at any time.

Months pass. Finally the interminable trial is over, and the Police Chief is sentenced to several years for his role in the conspiracy. The local Pagans decide that the sentencing of the Police Chief is an excellent cause for celebration. The evening is filled with bittersweet sorrow, because nothing will bring back their fallen comrade; yet they can rejoice that some degree of justice has at least been pursued. They pass the evening debating about the historical context of the goddesses Themis, Dike, and Justitia.

They also agree to organize another parade. This time, it's organized on a national level. They coordinate the event with covens and circles and houses and other various Pagan communities across the country. They ask all those groups to contact as many more groups and individual community members as they can, and try to organize everyone for a huge get-together. Listservs are started; social media accounts representing local event planners quickly gain hordes of followers.

And when the day arrives, an unprecedented number of Pagans march together in the streets: thousands upon thousands upon thousands. No one had even known that there are so many Pagans living in America. All across the country, Pagans walk together to raise their voices and proclaim their message.

The Oldest Religion is Back!

Appendix A: The Names of the Months

In the course of ironing out the details for their product line, the group's members are having a long conversation about their proposed calendar, including the names of the months, the dates of certain holidays, and even the names of the epochs of human history.

"The month names are problematic," comments Nicholas. "The Roman month names that we use are not all properly Pagan: they derive from the names of five deities, two emperors, and a bunch of boring numbers."

"Well," says Melissa, "if some of the months are named after gods, I think that's worth noting on our Pagan calendar. Which ones are they?"

"Well, January is named after the Roman goddess Janus. It was a conceptual association, because January is the first month, so you enter the year through it; and Janus was the goddess of doorways."

"That's beautiful," says Sage.

"The name February comes from the Latin word for purification."

"Purification?" asks Hayden.

"Sure," interjects Phoenix. "You didn't think Lent was originally a Christian holiday, did you? No, the idea of taking time for spiritual purification through austerities is common to many cultures; to the extent that Buddhism was initially a reaction against asceticism. In modern times, the Muslim holiday of Ramadan is the strictest ascetic observance; but the practice of spiritual purification has roots in the most ancient Pagan traditions, as you can see from the Roman name for the second month of the year."

"Especially since it followed a month of Saturnalia in December," comments Melissa.

"Anyway," Nicholas continues, "so the month of March is named for the god Mars. The spring month of April is probably named for Aphrodite, the goddess of love. May is, appropriately enough, named after the fertility goddess Maia. June, of course, is named for Juno, the queen of the Roman gods.

"But then Julius and Augustus were emperors, and the rest of the month names are just numbers. They're not even the correct numbers, because they got offset at some point; so the months named "eight" "nine" and "ten" are actually the tenth, eleventh, and twelfth months, respectively.[6]

"The point is, we only have good Pagan month names for the first half of the year."

"Personally," says Nicholas, "I like the Old English calendar, circa 700CE, as described by Bede. But we couldn't really just swap them out, because our modern calendar does not quite align with the lunar calendar of the ancients.

---

[6] The earliest Roman calendar began with March, and did not have any month names for the entire winter season, which existed as a sort of "time out of time." In a logical calendar reform, the months of January and February (whose name perhaps derives from an appellation for the god of death) were added at the beginning of the year, leaving the later months named after the wrong numbers; but the old names stuck. Two of those "number months" were eventually renamed in honor of the emperors Julius and Augustus. The Gregorian calendar slightly refined this system in 1582, leading to the calendar we still use to this day.

"Do you happen to know them offhand?" challenges Marc doubtfully.

"Yes, I do," replies Nicholas helpfully.

"Your knowledge of all things calendrical is quite astonishing," compliments Dylan.

"Thank you."

"Well, go on, do tell," Hayden presses. "What are the Old English names of the months?"

"Well, the month we call January was 'After Yule Month,' which the Saxons called 'Wolf Month.'

"The second month was 'Sol Month,' for the returning Sun; some called it 'Mud Month' or 'Cabbage Month.'

"The third month was 'Hretha Month,' named after a Pagan goddess. The Anglo-Saxons called it 'Lent Month.' The word 'Lent' derives from the Old German word for 'long,' because during the Pagan month of Lent, the days are getting longer in the run-up to the Vernal Equinox."

"I like it so far," says Diana.

"Great. Well, their April was 'Eostar Month,' named after the popular fertility goddess."

"The goddess of the radiant dawn," offers Sage.

"Then the fifth month was 'Three milkings month,' because the cows produce more milk per day at that time of year.

"This was followed by a two-moon long 'Traveling Month.' The Old English calendar was a lunar calendar, so it does not exactly correspond to our Gregorian calendar; but roughly speaking, their June was named 'Before Litha,' and July was named 'After Litha.' On leap years, they added an extra month in the middle, an entire month named Litha.

"Apparently, the name 'Litha' comes from the Old English word for gentle, navigable seas. If you had to go on a journey, this was the best time of year to do it, because the weather was clement and the seas were mild. In the Old English calendar, on leap years, Litha was inserted as an intercalary extra month, and then they would have a three-month long period called 'Before Litha,' 'Litha,' and 'After Litha.'"[7]

"However, other sources state that 'Litha' comes from the Old Norse, and that it simply means 'Long Day,' because the Summer Solstice is the longest day of the year. I haven't been able to determine which sources are correct.

"In fact there is some degree of uncertainty as to the earliest origin of the word, or which linguistic root the holiday takes its name from. It's all a bit lost to prerecorded history, to tell you the truth. Which egg came before the chicken? I don't know. Maybe someday a proper historian will answer the question.

"So that brings us to August. The Old English name was 'Weed month,' because that was the time of year you had to spend out in the garden under the hot sun, pulling weeds. The Celts named the entire month Lunasa, after the feast of the Sun God, Lugh.

---

7   It took me years to obtain a primary source to double-check this assertion. When I originally wrote *Rise of the Pagans*, the two most widely cited books on the subject were both out of print. They are, *Bede and Anglo-Saxon Paganism* by Audrey L. Meaney; and Faith Wallis's English-language translation of Bede's seminal work, *The Reckoning of Time*. The publisher of Wallis's book eventually ran another print run, and I was able to verify that Chapter 15 of Bede's *The Reckoning of Time*, written circa 730CE, does indeed include the Old English names of the months, as related in the present discussion. However, the month names as Bede recorded them do not distinguish between "before" and "after" the Solstices: they are simply two-month long periods named "Litha" and "Yule," respectively. I have let Nicholas's dialogue stand, because as a speaker, he knows only what I knew when I wrote the original version.

"The next month was 'Holy Month,' the sacred time of the harvest; known to the Saxons as 'Barley Month' for the same reason.

"Well, to the Old English Pagans, the year ended on Sowan, which they recognized as the beginning of Winter. So their October was named 'Winter Fylleth,' which means basically, 'The month in which winter begins on the first full moon.'

"So then November in Old English was the first month of the New Year; and they named it 'Blood Month,' because that's when the surplus livestock were sacrificed for the sake of continued prosperity through the coming winter. The Celts called this month 'Mi na Samhna,' or 'the month of Samhain,' beginning with the Sowan holiday, when gentle voices sound.

"And finally," Nicholas concludes, "the month we know as December, the Old English called it 'Before Yule Month.' So you can see, the Solstices were particularly important to the Old English calendar. Yule and Litha each had a two-month long period, divided into 'before' and 'after' the solstice event. No doubt this can be traced through the ancient Druidic traditions to the prehistoric Pagans who built Stonehenge."

"All right, that got a little long," says Melissa.

"It's all right," says Hayden. "I asked for it, I should have known..."

"Hey," says Nicholas, offended.

"No, seriously, I'm impressed you can remember all that," says Hayden hurriedly, trying to minimize the offense.

"And I'm still wondering," prompts Dennis, "which month names are we going to use for this calendar?"

"We could supply multiple choice options," suggests Diana. "One line could use the Roman versions for Janus through Juno, followed by simply, 'Month Seven,' 'Month

Eight,' and so on for the rest of the year. The next line could supply the more interesting of the Old English, Old Celt or Old Saxon month name."

"To Hades with two lines," says Phoenix. "One month name is enough. Just split the year down the middle: use the Roman origins for the first six months, and then the Old English names for the second half of the year."

"But I sure like 'Sol Month' better than 'Austerity Month,'" opines Hayden.

"Fine. We'll make an exception for February. So that leaves us with what, again?"

Dennis has been taking notes. He reads them off now. "That would be Janus, Sol, Mars, Aphrodite, Maia, Juno, After Litha, Weeding, Harvest, Winterfylleth, Blood Month, and Yule."

"It's a little weird," says Hayden. "But kind of cool."

"I like 'Wolf Month' and 'Mud Month' better, for the names of the first two months," offers Marc.

"They go well with 'Blood Month,'" Dylan agrees.

"I don't know," says Diana. "It starts to feel a bit dark. What if we keep Janus and Sol for the first two, but change 'Blood Month' to something else?"

"Sure," says Nicholas, who is thoroughly enjoying himself. "We could go with the old tradition of naming the month after that month's major holiday. So in our case, the eleventh month would be named 'Thanksgiving.'"

"That could cause confusion," objects Marc. "You'd be talking about the month, and people would think you were talking about the day."

"What about just a month named Thanks?" offers Melissa. "Then you'd have 31 days of Thanks."

"The month of Thanks," ponders Sage. "Now that is

really great. I love it."

"And let's use the Old Celtic name for the eighth month," Phoenix suggests.

"What if we continue the pattern of naming the month after its holiday?" offers Hayden. "Then we could name the sixth month 'Litha' and call the seventh month 'Juno.'"

"Yeah... I like it, conceptually," Phoenix begins diplomatically, "but a change like that would break our connection with broader society. I think the sixth month should be Juno because everyone calls it June. Once again, the purpose here is not to separate ourselves, but just to provide some context and tell a story about our people."

"It's just that naming a month 'After Litha' is so awkward," Hayden explains. "It's easier to say 'July.'"

"How about this," offers Dylan. "What if we use Ostara for the fourth month, instead of Aphrodite? It's more relevant to the holiday that's celebrated then."

"That's a good point," agrees Melissa. "Our calendar would become less Greco-Roman, but maybe that's appropriate."

"I don't know," Nicholas says hesitantly. "It doesn't really work to call the fourth month 'Ostar,' because Ostara Day, the Vernal Equinox, is generally the 21st day of the third month. The Abramist observation of Easter is the first Sun Day after the first full moon after the Vernal Equinox, which usually puts it in the fourth month; but properly speaking, Ostara is the Vernal Equinox itself. Flexible Pagans could celebrate a whole Eostarmonath spanning both dates; but for most of us, a week for spring break is the most we can muster."

"What does the group think?" asks Phoenix, who has grown bored because he is not the center of attention. "Group, we have two proposals for our calendar. One would use 'Ostara' for the fourth month, 'Litha' for the sixth month, and 'Juno' for the seventh month. The other plan uses 'Aphrodite' for the fourth month, 'Juno' for the sixth month, and 'After Litha' for the seventh month."

"Can't just call the seventh month Litha?" asks Hayden. "That would be easier."

"But it doesn't work because Litha occurs in the sixth month," replies Nicholas. "The seventh month is After Litha, hence the name."

"It's so awkward. Would you agree to a contraction? How about Aftlitha?"

"That's still a lot of consonants, if our purpose is simplicity of pronunciation."

"Just Alitha, then?"

"I admit, that is easier to say. A'litha, the month After Litha."

"Let's go with it for now," Phoenix jumps in, "and traditions can evolve later.

"All right," he continues, "so, group, the second proposal would call the fourth month 'Aphrodite,' the sixth month 'Juno,' and the seventh month 'Alitha.'

The second proposal wins by a wide margin.

Marc is not satisfied. "I'm still not sure," he says. "Remember, the stormy fall month of the ancient Celts was 'Sowan Month.' Maybe we could use 'Sowan' instead of 'Winterfylleth' for the tenth month."

"It's easier to say," agrees Hayden.

"I liked what you just said there," opines Sage.

"What, calling the tenth month 'Sowan?'"

"No, before that; you called it a 'stormy fall month.' What if we call it 'Stormfall?' It has the same feeling as 'Winterfylleth,' with the advantage of being more modern-sounding, and easier to pronounce. That would limit the number of times we name a month after the holiday. We don't want it to get too confusing."

"Does anyone still care about this?" asks Phoenix, eager to move on. "You get a seasonal reference either way. Thoughts?"

"Stormfall," calls out Hayden.

"There's a motion to use 'Stormfall' as the name of the tenth month on our calendar. Is there a second?"

"I'll second that," says Dennis. "It sounds like something out of George R. R. Martin."

"Motion is seconded. All in favor?"

A few people look up from their side conversations to quietly say "aye" or wave a hand to signal their approval.

"All opposed?"

They look around, but nobody says anything.

"The motion is carried. I move that the topic be closed."

A modest round of applause indicates that there is unanimous support for this final motion.

"All right, now I'm confused though," says Hayden. "Tell me one more time? What would that make it? What did we decide?"

Dennis reads from his notes: "The months of the year are Janus, Sol, Mars, Aphrodite, Maia, Juno, Alitha, Lunasa, Harvest, Stormfall, Thanks, and Yule."

"I'll buy that," says Phoenix with enthusiasm. "Sold. It's perfect. Those are the month names on our new Pagan calendar."

Dennis notes the final outcome of the discussion in his meeting minutes.

"Well," says Sage, "as long as we're providing alternate names for the months, what should we do about the years?"

"Hey, that's a good point," agrees Nicholas. "There's no need to continue to adhere to the Gregorian system which dates time from the birth of their Abramist man-god."

"But it's what everyone does," objects Marc. "The calendar has to agree with everyone's recognized system of numbering the years. Otherwise it won't make sense."

"The calendar should at least acknowledge that we live in the Common Era," says Phoenix. "All this *Anno Domini* stuff is more Abramist cultural imperialism. We need to remember that there's the time Before the Common Era (BCE), and then there's the Common Era (CE), which we live in now."

"Actually," offers Hayden, "we *can* adopt a more modern system of numbering the years, because we now live in the technology era. It's a new time for humanity. We could leave the Common Era behind."

People stare at him, and the room grows too quiet. He goes on and explains to the somewhat surprised group. "Computer programmers already have a new beginning of historical time: January 1, 1970. It's called the Unix Epoch. It's already an internationally recognized standard. And really, if your argument about having a universal calendar is that you need it for business purposes, what could be more forward-looking for business purposes than integrating the modern calendar with your computer's timestamp function? It actually makes more sense this way.

"So," he concludes, "our new Pagan calendars would number the years since the Unix Epoch began. If 1970 is year 0, then 1980 is year 10, 1990 is year 20; the year 2000 becomes year 30; 2010 was year 40; and 2020 will be year 50 of the Unix Epoch."

"Yeah," says Marc sarcastically. "All we need to do is get historians to divide time into three segments: the time Before the Common Era; the time of the Common Era, which lasted for 1,969 years; and the new Modern Era, which began at the time of the Unix Epoch."

"That might take some persuasion," Nicholas agrees, "to get them to see it from that perspective. But we could hurry the process along by talking about it, and spreading the idea. We could even get them to define a new name for the two thousand or so years immediately preceding the Common Era. They could officially divide recorded history into three phases: Classical Antiquity, the Common Era, and the Unix Epoch."

"I think you're stretching now," Marc maintains.

"We'll see," says Hayden, and begins flipping through some of the reference books gathered there.

"Actually," interjects Sage, "if you're talking about renumbering the years for the Pagan calendar, there's no need to start a new system. There's already a magical calendar devised by Aleister Crowley that has its own very specific way of enumerating the months and the years."

"Ah, yes," says Nicholas, "the Thelemic Calendar."

"I'm not familiar with the Thelemic Calendar," says Dylan. "What is it?"

"The Thelemic Calendar references the astrological positions of the sun and the moon instead of the month and the day," explains Sage. "So instead of saying, 'Today is November 23', you would say, 'Today the sun is in 1 degree Sagittarius, and the moon is in 12 degrees Leo.' And the years are counted from the date of Mr. Crowley's great mystical revelation."

"Oh, it gets even more complicated," interrupts Nicholas, who loves to talk about calendars. "The Thelemic year is written as a pair of Roman numerals, based on a 22-year cycle. So the first number in the pair counts the 22-year cycles since

Crowley started writing his book in 1904; and the second number in the pair counts the number of years since the beginning of the present 22-year cycle."

"Why 22 years?" Hayden wants to know.

"Who cares?" explodes Marc. Hayden shrinks back from the sudden ferocity. "Look," Marc goes on, "I only have two problems with the Thelemic calendar as you describe it. The first is, astrology is total bullshit, okay? The random patterns made by the relative positions of distant suns absolutely, definitively, do not in any way shape or form influence my life at all, even in the slightest."

"You sound just like a Taurus," says Sage.

"You already know my birthday, and it doesn't fucking matter anyway!" Marc rages. "I am not assigned a destiny by the date of my birth! I am a free man! I possess self-awareness, and the capacity for self-determination! I am not fated to be who I am by birth order, constellations, or fucking tea leaves!"

"There's no need to get upset about it," says Sage.

"And furthermore," Marc goes on, ignoring her, "Aleister Crowley was an egotistical piece of shit. I reject his teachings, as I reject him personally. I refuse to countenance a calendar that numbers the years of the modern era as dating since the day he first stuck his thumb up his own ass hole."

A shocked silence follows this enraged outburst of profanity. Eventually Melissa pipes up, "Well, that's one vote against using the Thelemic Calendar. Does anybody else feel strongly about this?"

Nobody else does, and the group's eventual calendar does not incorporate Gnostic mysticism, Thelemic teachings, or even the positions of the signs of the Zodiac.

Meanwhile, Hayden is examining a list of the names and

dates of the Pagan Sabbats. "I don't know," he says, changing the subject. "I think these popular books on Pagan practice are wrong. Immolc should be on the first day of the month of February; not the second."

"You think the books are all wrong?" says Melissa quizzically.

"Yeah, I mean, look. The solstices and equinoxes form the quarters, and we observe them at the time of specific solar events. But by convention, the cross-quarters are observed at the beginning or the end of a month. You've got Beltane on May 1, Lammas on August 1, and Sowan on October 31 because it's an ending day. Logically, Immolc should be celebrated on February 1."

"Well," Nicholas replies, "properly speaking, the cross-quarters should be exactly midway between the solstices and the equinoxes. So if you wanted to get pedantic about it, their dates should move according to the fluctuations of the solar year."

"Maybe we should start a new system."

"That's a great idea," retorts Marc, his face still red, "but nobody would purchase a calendar that disagrees with the existing tradition, and we're trying to make money here."

"It's worth a thought anyway," Hayden maintains defensively.

"Sure," agrees Phoenix diplomatically. "For now, while I think you have a valid point, I'm going to have to agree with Marc on this one." At this, Marc visibly relaxes. "The fact is," continues Phoenix, "there is an established community that's already in the habit of observing Immolc on the second day of February."

"Really?" Hayden isn't quite ready to let it go. "Isn't this the one Sabbat that our friends always seem to forget about? I think putting it on the first day of the month would make it more memorable."

"Fine, but do you really want to alienate the Pagan community, which is the target market for this calendar?"

Always the peacemaker, Sage speaks up. "What if we marked a proper solar calculation for Immolc, based on the midpoint between the Winter Solstice and the Vernal Equinox, but then wrote it on the second day of the second month as 'Immolc (observed)?'"

This motion is carried and adopted. And with it, the modern Pagan calendar is established.

Appendix B: An Atheist Book of Psalms

Prayer of the Questing One

O enlightenment, fill me with understanding
   that I may see the right path

The Litha Hale-Bopp Eclipse

What is wrong, what is right
    the longest day, the shortest night
We get down on our knees and play
    the shortest night, the longest day
Once I saw a comet in the sky
    the ancients would have thought
        we were about to die
Because true as these words fall from my lips
    that night there was also a lunar eclipse
All on the Summer Solstice
    the axis point of the seasons
We celebrate the Summer Solstice
    for a thousand beautiful reasons

The Sabbat Dance

This is a day of power
        a nexus of solar convergence
So join with me to celebrate
        let us join in the dance

Finding the Path

O goodness for which we strive
        for the betterment of self and all
Fill our hearts with sacred light
        and drive out darkness therein
May we find peace
        and turn away from anger
May we be forgiving
        in the face of the wickedness of men
For through our understanding we may bring
        a better world to come to pass

A Blessing

In the name of all that is beautiful
in the name of all we hold dear
in the name of our communal togetherness
bestow our blessings upon this event.

Convergence

We celebrate
	our hearts fill with joy
		glad to be present at such a moment
Events converge
	the planets align
		an auspicious time

The Voices of the Gods

Tinkling small sounds
        cascading and radiating
Leaves on the trees
        whispering in the breeze

Praise

Praise be to natural systems
Glory be to all
The interconnectedness of energy and matter
        from subatomic particles to
                the whirling motion of galaxies
Praise all
Praise all

Asking Forgiveness

May my transgressions be forgiven
　　though I know I have done wrong
I vow to learn from my mistakes
　　to make such atonement as may be made
And to lead my life henceforth purposefully
　　putting past evils behind me
Setting my eyes upon the
　　attainment of balance

Notes & Resources

My thanks go out to the many friends and community members who shared their insights and information about the many ways to celebrate the Old Ways and the Goddess. This book would not have been possible without you.

Special thanks go out to local Pagan scholar Jon "Armadel" Rigby, who not only performed several life-changing introductions, he also originated the chant, "This time is not a time / This place is not a place," and if I'd realized that at the time, I'd have given him a lyric-writing credit on the song "The Ritual" from the debut Flumergex album, "This One." The character of Nicholas is not intended to represent Jon; but I admit that there might be some similarities.

My thanks to Ryan Casper for sharing many insights, especially pertaining to Gardnerian tradition and the circle ritual; and for passing the mead horn with me.

Thanks to Moon St. Clair and his family for keeping the Solstices and Equinoxes alive in Lewis County, you guys first started me thinking like a Pagan.

Thanks to my friends from my St. Andrews days, who dragged me to that wild and memorable Beltane festival on the hilltop overlooking Edinburgh in 1996. "Pants!"

Thanks to Joe Tackett and Carmella Cook for spreading the word and staying devoted to the cause.

Thanks to the Shadowluz coven for being welcoming and inclusive.

Thanks to all my family members for your love and support, and for putting up with me. Thanks especially to my Mom for raising me in a tradition of Winter Solstice bonfires, and for Kokopelli-rich trips to the desert Southwest and even remoter locales.

A huge thanks to my sister, Lindsey LaRock, my fellow Stonehenge ape, for her detailed review of my draft manuscript. Lindsey has earned editor credit for her work; and I want it known that I accepted most of her suggestions. I appreciate it, thank you!

And many thanks to my beautiful wife, Dr. Jessica Lehrfeld, for advice and information, for reading drafts that weren't ready to be read, and for our family, the hope and promise of the future.

You're all awesome, and I think of you more than I say.

Additionally, this book was informed and influenced by the following reference materials.

Joseph Campbell and Bill Moyers. (1988). *The Power of Myth*. New York, NY: Doubleday.

Vere Chappell. (n.d.). *Thelemic Calendar and Holidays*. Retrieved from http://www.thelema101.com/calendar

Susan Cooper. (1973). *The Dark is Rising*. New York, NY: Aladdin Paperbacks. [Cooper is the source for the footnote about a traditional Yule log being the split root of a beech tree. While her book is a work of fantasy fiction, the passage about the Yule log has the ring of traditional truth, so I have included the reference here.]

Russell Cottrell. (2013). *Celtic Date and Moon Phase*. Retrieved from http://russellcottrell.com/celticDate

Ingri and Edgar Parin D'Aulaire. (1967). *D'Aulaires' Book of Norse Myths: Preface by Michael Chabon.* New York, NY: The New York Review of Books.

Ingri and Edgar Parin D'Aulaire. (1962). *Ingri and Edgar Parin D'Aulaire's Book of Greek Myths.* Garden City, NY: Doubleday & Company, Inc.

Patrick K. Ford (translator, editor). (1977). *The Mabinogi and other Welsh Tales.* Berkeley, CA: University of California Press.

Steven J. Gibson. (n.d.). *Common Holidays in Relation to Equinoxes, Solstices & Cross-Quarter Days.* Retrieved from http://www.naic.edu/~gibson/cal

Alma Guillermoprieto. (May 12, 2013). *Vatican in a Bind about Santa Muerte.* National Geographic. Retrieved from http://news.nationalgeographic.com/news/2013/13/130512-vatican-santa-muerte-mexico-cult-catholic-church-cultures-world

Fergus Fleming, Shahrukh Husain, C. Scott Littleton, and Linda A. Malcor (1996). *Heroes of the Dawn: Celtic Myth and Mankind.* Amsterdam, Holland: Time Life Books.

Prudence Jones and Nigel Pennick. (1995). *A History of Pagan Europe.* New York, NY: Barnes & Noble Books. [Highly recommended, well written and painstakingly researched.]

George R. R. Martin. (1999). *A Clash of Kings.* New York, NY: Bantam Books. [Fans of the "Game of Thrones" series will recognize Martin as the inspiration for Hayden's internal monologue about boar hunting.]

Dr. Sam Newton. (2000). "The Old English Calendar." *Wuffing's Website.* Retrieved from http://www.wuffings.co.uk/OECalendar.htm

Pagan Calendar. (2013). *Pagan Calendar.* Retrieved from http://www.pagancalendar.co.uk [I couldn't find the names of the people who run this website, but it packs a lot of good information into a small space.]

Plutarch, with Charles W. Eliot (editor). (1959). *Plutarch's Lives of Themistocles, Pericles, Aristedes, Alcibiades and Coriolanus, Demosthenes and Cicero, Caesar and Antony, In the translation called Dryden's, corrected and revised by Arthur Hugh Clough, with introduction and notes.* The Harvard Classics, Volume 12. New York, NY: P.F. Collier & Son Corporation. [Plutarch's detailed descriptions of the Lupercalia festival corrected my previous incorrect impression that it was a city-wide public orgy.]

J.M. Robertson. (1903). *Pagan Christs.* New York, NY: Dorset Press. [This edition is a reprint, dated 1987. Please note that while Robertson has done excellent research, especially considering the concept and practice of sacrifice, I ultimately disagree with his fundamental premise. It's my personal opinion that many mythological heroes, demigods, and godheads, notably Jesus and Buddha, almost certainly began as stories about actual people.]

Donna Rosenberg (editor). (1989). *World Mythology: An Anthology of the Great Myths and Epics.* Lincolnwood, IL: Passport Books. [Includes a translation of The Epic of Gilgamesh, as well as a version of the myth of Deucalion and Pyrrha.]

Sir Walter Scott. (1820). *Ivanhoe.* [This is the source of the incantation spoken by Sage at the conclusion of the memorial service for Phoenix. I transcribed the verse from the 1997 BBC/A&E 6-part miniseries production of Scott's novel.]

Starhawk, Diane Baker, and Anne Hill. (1998). *Circle Round: Raising Children in Goddess Traditions.* New York, NY: Bantam Books. [Starhawk aka Miriam Simos.]

Starhawk. (1989). *The Spiral Dance: A Rebirth of the Ancient Religion of the Great Goddess (10th anniversary ed).* San Francisco,

CA: Harper & Row Publishers.

Star Sapphire Lodge. (2013). *Thelemic Calendar Conversion.* Retrieved from http://www.starsapphire-oto.org/calendar.jsp

Faith Wallis (translator). (2012 edition). *Bede: The Reckoning of Time, Translated, with introduction, notes and commentary by Faith Wallis.* Liverpool, UK: Liverpool University Press. [Footnote 7 explains the importance of this reference. It's an impressive work!]

H.G. Wells. (1971). *The Outline of History: Being a Plain History of Life and Mankind, Volumes One and Two (Revised and brought up to date by Raymond Postgate and G.P. Wells).* Garden City, New York: Doubleday & Company, Inc. [Wells is not a very good historian; and portions of the original manuscript are known to have been plagiarized. Despite these flaws, the perspective Wells sets forth here is definitely worth a read. This appears to be the fourth edition, and was published posthumously. The first edition was published in 1920.]

Wikipedia. (2013). *Wikipedia.* Retrieved from http://en.wikipedia.org/wiki/Wheel of the Year and others. [I consulted many Wikipedia entries, especially concerning the names of the months and the logic of the Gregorian calendar; but also some word origins, points of historical fact, and even the astronomical symbols used in the front cover design. Wikipedia is an invaluable resource.]

William Butler Yeats (editor) and Lady Isabella Augusta Gregory (translator) with Claire Booss (compilation). (1986). *A Treasury of Irish Myth, Legend, and Folklore: Fairy and Folk Tales of the Irish Peasantry, and Cuchulain of Muirthemne: The Story of the Men of the Red Branch of Ulster.* Avenel, NJ: Gramercy Books. [Lady Gregory's text helpfully describes the derivation of the old Gaelic names for four of the Sabbats.]

9 780097 664238 1